Diary of a house move

Deborah Fielding

Published in 2012 by FeedARead Publishing

British Library C.I.P.

A CIP catalogue record for this title is available from the British Library.

To my wonderful husband and partner in crime.

With thanks to

Carl and Tamara Buckler

For their kindness and patience in designing the front and back cover for me.

January

Depersonalise and de-clutter

Get rid of any rubbish now, charity shops will be grateful and put things away in storage or to understanding friends or family, either way make sure you seal the boxes.

Tuesday 1 January

During a mince pie and mulled wine bonanza over the Christmas holidays, Husband and I have decided that we wanted to move house again. This time we agreed everything would work out perfectly, i.e. not take the house off the market again and actually move out.

Oh my God. It has to work out.

I will call some agents for valuations as soon as their offices re-open after the Christmas holidays. Not that we need a valuation, have looked so much on-line at property types and prices they are on for, feel I already know our house price. We sit down with left over selection boxes and mince pies to compile a list which we will stick to when looking for houses.

Dream house wish list
- detached
- country/quiet location
- en-suite/cloaks
- large garden
- safe garden for disabled dog and cat
- parking
- larger rooms
- views
- utility (ironing room)
- not on a busy/main road
- have some character/old

Can't think any more, it seems we have overdosed on sugar and e-numbers. We leave the list as it is for now and put a new DVD on to watch and raid the Quality Street again as levels are quickly dipping.

Monday 7 January

Ring three agents today and make appointments for valuations. Why have we had to wait so long for Estate Agents to open, it's not like they do anything when they are in their offices so they could just sit there eating mince pies and opening their presents at their desks, staying open all of the holidays.

Discover a site online to check house prices. It shows what a property was last sold for. This could come in useful for past sales and knocking a price down when offering.

I spent hours trawling through house sites on-line for suitable properties and areas. Couldn't believe how many houses were built in the 1960s in our desired location. Most of them look like village halls or doctor's surgeries. Yuck. They seem to have massive panes of glass for windows and wood, brick and stone all mixed up for the house exterior.

No character properties at all. It's like the whole of this area was developed in the 1960s. Could we extend or renovate ugly houses and maybe make some money on them in order to sell on for a character property which we would prefer?

Probably not. Something is bound to go wrong. We'd probably end up stuck in a doctor's surgery for life. It would end up being a vehicle into the afterlife.

Find a selling guide on-line and print out to read. First title 'How to choose the right agent'. The guide goes on about asking family, friends and colleagues for references in order to find excellent estate agents. Do any agents come with a glowing reference or is it basically down to the colour of their tie or suit on the day they visit you, if you like it or not?

There is also a buying guide which we look through. The guide says that buying a property is a big step which you have to think hard about, also, can you afford it blah, blah, blah. It's all we have thought about. What is clever is the budget calculator we find. I get carried away with checking all sorts of figures; Husband sees me doing this and promptly puts me right. Also look at a mortgage calculator. Again, I start looking at really expensive houses until Husband puts me right again. I send him off in to the garden.

It's serious business buying and selling houses, need to focus. It's all a joke really – I seem to be slipping into a different reality where the sky is full of flying animals and money is floating away down the stream of life!

Wednesday 9 January

First valuation is due today at 10am. House is tidy and clean, all ready for agents to have a nosey round. Cleaning was carried out like a precision military action. From top to bottom and then sideways, just in case I missed anything. Shame it doesn't look like this for us all of the time.

Note to self
- clean more often
- take dog to the vets for booster jab and to check her eyes (she seems to be bumping into things)

Agent turned up on time wearing a smart suit and driving a fancy car. Very polite though, quite likeable.

The dog decided to get up. She doesn't usually get up for us. She walked over to agent and casually stretched up his leg for a fuss and then casually wandered off to knock her food bowl about leaving white hair neatly arranged on the agent's suit trouser leg making it look like he had yeti boots on.

Agent said lovely house etc, blah, blah, blah. Our house was valued less than we thought so it looks like we can only afford a doctor's surgery house after all. Character properties need to be stricken from the list. They are way out of our budget. Unless we can raise enough cash selling off unwanted Christmas presents.

Note to self

- Check E-Bay for selling unwanted gifts and any crap we have left in the loft.
- Check on-line to see if can make animals super stars for looking cute.

Thursday 10 January

I am waging a campaign to find the perfect house and trawl the house sites on-line again. Decide to make appointments to view a few doctors' surgeries. Ask in laws along to some viewings for their opinion/help. Maybe they could spot something disastrous which we might miss. Download and print off brochures for the houses we are viewing at the weekend. They have magnificent pictures and very grand wordings. I can only assume that it is a fellow literary colleague who has written them.

Three viewings arranged for the weekend with them. Looking forwards to seeing some houses in the flesh after just looking at pictures on-line.

Note to self
- Clean house for tomorrow's valuation
- Feed dog before she knocks her bowl through to next door in a temper

Friday 11 January

Second valuation is today at 12 noon. Another military action taking place today, I clean and tidy the house in the morning. It's the second time this week, must be a world record.

Oh my God!

The valuer turned up on time and was friendly but the valuation was £30-35k less than we had thought. Maybe we could just afford to buy a caravan now. Maybe increase mortgage slightly if we want a static one. As the Housemartin's song goes, it could be our 'Caravan of Love'.

Note to self
-    get a job.......

Nip out and buy the local paper which has the housing section in for our area. Waste of money. Maybe dog could eat newspaper instead of dog biscuits to save money on pet food.

Saturday 12 January

Weekend is here. Lots of fun lies ahead of us. Blooming marvellous. A viewing has been made for today. A traditional 3 bed detached house. Nice on the outside, time warp on the inside. Oh my God! There are wallpaper and patterned carpets galore. Maybe a pub in its past life? A real doctor's surgery would definitely be decorated better than this. Nice big garden though, not too overlooked, not that I am planning to do anything in the garden where people would want to watch me anyway. Unless there are weirdoes nearby who like to look at undies on the washing line. You never know.

It was an accompanied viewing. Agent came to show us around, must have had a personally bypass. She was heavily made up with the usual grey suit on with big hair and lots of bling. She parked in the middle of the drive leaving no room for us so we had to park on the road in a junction. She also went around closing all of the internal doors as soon as we left each room. On a couple of occasions I could feel a huge draft on the back of my neck. She couldn't find the keys for the back door. In the end we just looked at back garden through the window. Made all the right sounds but when Husband and I looked at each other we knew it wasn't the one. This is just as well because she was locking the front door behind us with no chance of another quick look around. It is a Saturday after all.

Sunday 13 January

Half the weekend has gone now. Still not found a house. Have three viewings today with the in-laws. Wonder what we will all think of the prospective properties?

Oh my God! Rewind to the 60s/70s/80s in décor and you wouldn't be disappointed. You could set a BBC drama in them. It is amazing that between all of the property programmes that are around on the TV, not one owner has watched them and improved their own houses. Where are these improved properties anyway? Not in our area that's for sure. How come people think their houses are worth so much when they've not been touch with the magic decorating brush in decades?

In-laws were not very helpful. Would call them well-wishers really, as in they don't wish us very much harm. All they did was talk about themselves to the vendor while we looked around. Back in the car their comments include, 'nice garden, kitchen needs doing though.' Very helpful. Couldn't have worked this out without them. Thanks.

Out of the three houses, one seems to stand out more than the others. It's one that we actually viewed last year when people were living in it. The family selling it have come to let us in to have a look around because it is now empty. Still a 60's throwback but something could be done with it. It has double garage for Husband, kitchen diner for me, 4 beds, big garden and room to extend. Funnily enough we had the same wallpaper but in a different colour way in our first house. Maybe it's a sign. Nope, only thing this tells us it that we have lived in our present house 11 years now so when we papered the previous house it was yonks ago, so the wallpaper is definitely now dated. We called this house Father's because it had belonged to the vendor's father who had died, hence being empty. Hopefully he didn't die in the house. Wouldn't want an old man ghost bumping around in the night, have enough with noise from the disabled dog and half blind cat.

When we looked around it last year it was summer, very hot. The woman was preparing food in the kitchen for dinner and kindly let us look around her house on our own. When we got to the top of the stairs a really strong poo smell hit us as we pushed the first door open. Oh my God! There was a full nappy bag stinking out all of the upstairs. It had been left on the changing table. I'm sure I could see a swarm of flies approaching from a Northerly direction. We both retched and fled from the room shutting the door firmly behind us. The rest of the viewing was a blur because our eyes had been burnt. Did they want to sell the house or not?

Note to self
- go to viewings on our own
- feed dog before she eats her bowl, maybe dog could become famous and earn loads of money doing tricks with her food bowl?

Tuesday 15 January

Third 'no obligation' valuation today at 1.30pm. Need a sit down. I have just cleaned the house again. I must find somewhere to hide a pile of ironing before they come. The car boot turns out very useful for all kinds of crap to hide. Husband and I think we have decided which agents we are going with but are having a third valuation because we are told it is the proper thing to do.

Agents rang to say they will be late. Twice. Does 'no obligation' mean no obligation to turn up? Told them that we would leave it and thanked them, (didn't really mean any niceness). Will stick with the other two valuations and decide from them. What a waste of time this morning has been. Remind me again, why?

Is there actually an estate agent that does what it says?

Note to self
- never trust what anyone says when they are wearing a flash suit and have an expensive car parked outside making the neighbours wonder what you are up to.

Take the dog to the vets for her booster jab. Use the waiting time wisely and browse the pet shop attached to the vets. They stock some wonderful foods if you're a dog. Decide on a pig's ear together for the dog and hear the vets call our name as we are paying. Good timing for a change. They give the dog an MOT and check her eyes. She has something wrong with them. Her eyes are constantly moving from side to side. Poor thing. Maybe we could call back in the shop and buy her something else? Maybe a lovely new collar or a delightful pink t-shirt? Have we got to cover everything at dog level in bubble wrap to stop her bumping in to things? At least any viewers might think we have started packing early.

Wednesday 16 January

Have been busy today. Looked at a barn conversion this morning. It was nice. Ticks most of the boxes but the only thing it had against it was that it was attached at both sides to other conversions. Damn. Still ask though if the builder has considered a part-exchange. Has a small garden. Probably not big enough for the dog and it will need a wall building to keep her in. The rooms are large and the kitchen is a gorgeous distressed white French style. There isn't a garage, only a drive for one car and a car port on the edge of the small estate. This leaves us wondering where we would put all of our crap which is currently residing in our garage. It seems weird only having one door on the front. No back door, no side door. At least it has views over the countryside and is quiet.

Need to think about this. Doctor's surgery versus brand new interior and very old exterior?

It seems worth considering because we go away and work out some figures. On the way home we pass McDonalds and call in for a latte. A caffeine boost may help us think.

Friday 18 January

Pick up local paper with house section in. Found a builder in our considered area with a small development. Newspaper is worth its money this week. Will not feed it to dog. Can't anyway, dog has knocked her bowl so hard into the kitchen cupboard it needs surgically removing.

Drove to small development and found out number of beds, prices etc. Chuff me, how much? They have put the most snobbiest bitch in the portacabin looking after the site; she decided that we couldn't afford the houses she was flogging by looking at our casual clothes. Sorry love but appearances can be deceptive. Wonder if you could afford these houses looking at your old car parked up on the driveway?

Do they really think a 4/5 bed house will sell for £200k more than an average house price in the area because they are new? After talking to the sales negotiator we find out that builders are struggling selling them. She didn't actually say this. Husband and I worked it out for ourselves when we found out they were offering 105% part exchange, stamp duty paid and solicitor's fees paid. It is still not worth it though.

Wonder if the stuck up bitch will sell any houses anyway with her attitude? She didn't even ask us if we wanted a coffee, thought she had a superb show house with a hundred newly invented appliances in the kitchen.

Asked if we could look around the show house because the other houses weren't yet built. She was very insistent that we take our shoes off or cover our feet with those little plastic blue sock things. As my feet were cocooned within my knee high boots I decided to be stylish and put on the blue sock things. This seemed to please her as she gave me a satisfied nod. I felt as if I needed to crawl around the house on my hands and knees like a Crime Scene Investigator with a magnifying glass. Felt like a right twat. Husband got a disapproving glare when he slipped his trainers off to reveal grubby socks with several holes in them. He didn't notice her though as he was already halfway up the stairs looking for an appropriate PlayStation room.

The rooms were quite small and there were lots of them. Why not make less of them but big enough for a double bed and a wardrobe? You couldn't even brush your teeth in the en-suite without banging your bum on the wall and head butting the taps when rinsing your mouth. We take the information she is branding and disappear.

Buy some home magazines on the way home and discover a very useful website, www.upmystreet.com.

It tells you different things about areas you may be considering moving to. Very interesting. Didn't realise that our prospective housing area is quite possibly the crime capital of the world.

Saturday 19 January

Best to start the weekend off with a viewing. It's the second viewing on one of the three which we viewed with in laws. It has better kitchen units than the nicer house of the three but it doesn't detract from being a small room and still not to my taste. Husband likes the double garage and it is already fenced in on the back for the dog with minimum steps for her to fall down. Remind me. Why did we view this one again?

I don't get the feeling in my head or heart. The vendor had her ironing board set up upstairs on the landing in the large window, with clothes placed around like a laundrette. Couldn't see out of the window or get passed without knocking piles of clothes over.

Is she trying to sell her house or start a laundry business? Maybe a laundry business will finance her move?

Note to self
- make a list of things to do, still not chosen an agent to go to market with.

Although, if looking at new houses with part exchanges that pay for estate agents do we wait?

Saturday 26 January

Spent all week looking for houses on-line. Found a good site though. www.rightmove.co.uk is the best to use for me because it is so easy. Can find new or used houses. Although sill nothing new, everything boring. Why are there no castles available to buy?

Got to tidy the garden so it looks presentable for viewers when we go to market. Either with an agent or a part exchange, still not decided. However, I am determined the garden will look spring like in winter and all the dog poo picked up and disposed of. Where are my asbestos gloves and carrier bags? If this is what she does with her food maybe feed her less?

Decided we need some new plants to pretty up the flower beds and the strategically placed pots. Maybe some fresh bark chippings for the front garden. Maybe paint the garage door again. Oh, don't want to forget to paint the fence. Oh my God. I have read far too many articles in home magazines. Flower beds already brimming with bright plants and shrubs.

Still go to B&Q anyway just to check what they have.

Big mistake. Everyone seems to have had the same idea. Crap. Crazy queues at every till. Husband is chuntering like he's got Tourettes. He says something like, 'do we really need this stuff?' and is about to dump the trolley when the queue seems to miraculously disappear.

We call for a latte on the way home. Need sustenance quick. Spend the rest of the afternoon tending the garden, again, making use of the new plants by updating the pots and flower beds.

The dog decides to help by digging up a flower bed on the patio. Thanks dog. She is now covered in damp soil and needs a bath badly. She seems pleased with herself though.

Sunday 27 January

Again, amazingly enough the housing section in the local paper has come up trumps. Found another new house site a few miles out of our desired area. Husband and I go along to check it out. Oh my God. Cars parked everywhere because the builders haven't put in big enough driveways. It's like a slalom down to the show house. The show house is beautiful though. When we look inside I can't help myself and I have to stroke the silk curtains and feel envious. Although we notice straight away that the furniture is all child sized to ensure spacious rooms. At least the internal doors have been left on. In one show house we looked round they had all been removed to make the small rooms seem bigger. What twats the house builders are.

Big 4 bed houses, double garages, reasonable price, extras like refrigerators, dishwashers etc but postage stamp gardens. Talking to lovely sales negotiator. Oh my God! What is that noise? 'It's just the train on the tracks behind the estate, it runs quite regularly. It's the main line to London,' she replies with a shrug.

The lovely sales negotiator had a personality, shame about the site. The houses were big and lovely though.

February

Tidy cupboards

This is where you will have shoved all of your rubbish when tidying and viewers will look in all cupboards. In food cupboards get rid of any tins or packets with old sell by dates because it's not worth paying the removal men to take them to the new house.

Sunday 3 February

Oh my God!

A month has passed. No house on the horizon to buy and move into and ours is still not on the market. Crap.

Another week spent surfing the internet and driving around areas we like looking for new for sale boards popping up. Spending a fortune on coffee. We started with lattes and we are now beginning to need it stronger, extra shots of espressos and sugar are on the menu. May have to reduce the budget for a house.

Have put off signing up with an agent because of looking at new houses with part exchanges.

Note to self
- Brush the dog and trim her fringe
- Ring carpet cleaners for lounge/dining room/stairs/hallway

It is evening time and there is nothing on the TV so we cruise around in the car looking for new sale boards. Need to start wearing hats and dark glasses to disguise ourselves. People might think we are stalkers or peeping toms. Eventually see a new board. Things are looking up. An old stone property which is detached. On the downside, it is next to a primary school.

All I can see when I close my eyes are screaming children and 4x4 yummy mummy's galore. Maybe an odd football through the kitchen window which overlooks the playground every so often. But somehow the lure of a character property is too much, the neighbours will have to do. We need to make an appointment to view it.

Monday 4 February

Ring first thing to arrange a viewing with old property we saw last night. Looked round it this afternoon. It was an accompanied viewing. Old man let us wander around and didn't follow us. He sat on a deep windowsill reading a book in the lounge. He was much nicer than the other agent on the accompanied viewing who closed all the doors behind us and had a personality bypass.

So far so good. Old double fronted character house with period details, detached, large garden ...... goes downhill now. No kitchen, next to a school, and a footpath runs alongside of the property. Three bedrooms but the bathroom is reached through the smallest bedroom. It will need some walls moving around to modernise it. Some features, coving, high ceilings and high skirting boards. The road is quite close to the front of the property which means traffic will be rattling the front windows and probably more. Do we need to look for big cracks in the stonework? The Church is selling it. It will probably go to sealed bids and end up going to a builder. We decide to offer on it anyway. It serves us right. Time to sit back and wait now.

Decide to get a coffee; we really need a caffeine fix and end up drawing plans for extensions and improvements for this character property on napkins.

Note to self
- Really must take a notebook with us

Friday 8 February

Make a list of things to do. Can't do housework am far too busy and important making a list.

Jobs to do to sell home faster
- Decide on a reasonable price to ask for it (don't want to over price it or look desperate)
- Check for any small jobs to do
- Make a small jobs list for Husband
- Do we need to redecorate to sell?
- Is the front of the house tidy?
- Clear clutter

Jobs to do
- Re-grout bathroom tiles
- Paint garden fence
- Put some plant pots at the front door with beautiful, eye catching designer arrangements in them
- Paint chipped radiator in the dining room
- Get garden furniture out of shed to stage the patio
- Cut grass
- Take clutter and crap to mum in laws to make rooms seem more spacious

That's enough for now. Need a rest, sit down with a home magazine for new decorating ideas for next house. Decide to pop out and buy local paper for housing section.

There is a new property in the paper. A property in the chosen area. Ring up and make an appointment to view. The vendors can actually make tomorrow. Excellent. Need a backup property as the character property will end up with someone else who can throw money at it during the renovation work.

Saturday 9 February

Things are looking up slightly. Then again......

We are viewing the new on the market property today. Oh my God it is another dormer bungalow. It's not on our dream list. We are looking at it because of location. Husband and I try and make it work in our minds as we are looking around it. Changes that could be made and changes that must be made. It is on a big plot though. Could it be knocked down and rebuilt into a proper house? No, can't afford that.

All of the interior is dated, needs new kitchen, bathrooms x2 and the layout changing to suit us.

We can afford to buy the house but then we would have no money left over for all of the improvements we want to make. Don't know if I could get used to the very strange layout.

Husband likes it though. It reminds him of a James Bond house. Oh, it has also got a double garage which has an internal door into the dining room. Oh, it also has an electric door. It appears to have a driveway similar to a helicopter landing pad. He seems pleased. Looking around the property both vendors followed us and then shut all doors behind us. The only dormer bedroom was cladded out in loads of orange pine, it felt like a cheap Swedish sauna. Although only guessing at this as I haven't been in a cheap Swedish sauna. And to our surprise there was also a telescope set up looking out of the window. Husband whispered something about locking the perverts up for spying on their neighbours. When questioned about said object the vendors said there was a good view of the local church. Ok then. When we were on the patio and they were explaining about the pond, Husband walked to the other side of the pond to look in and they more or less sprinted after him. Don't know what they thought he would do. It hasn't been a lifelong ambition of his to swim with fish/dolphins so I couldn't really say. Maybe he was looking at them for a fish supper?

Thought we might have heard about the offer we put in on the lovely, kitchen less character house earlier in the week. Nothing as yet.

We do know that there is an open viewing on this character property tomorrow though. Crap. Looks like it will be sealed bids. Crap a doodle.

Go for café mocha, it is the weekend after all.

Note to self
- need to look at purchasing lovely coffee machine, it would be cheaper in the long run than buying out all of the time

Sunday 10 February

Open viewing on the character house today. It takes ages to get to viewing time. We go along to see how much interest there was on it. Oh my God! 47 different viewers, all had to sign in, we know this because we counted every name. Cars were parked in every available nook and cranny. Was like bees round a particularly large, oozing honey pot. Things are not going our way. Need to stop imagining where our furniture will go.

We've already offered on this! It's so annoying that they keep showing viewers around. It will definitely go to a builder. They are always willing to throw money at houses which they think will make them a fortune to sell on. People are touching our beautiful feature fireplaces and walls, peeling up the wallpaper to look at the walls behind it. Stop it!

Couples of all sizes and ages are wandering around with someone's kids running and skidding around everyone. Try to trip some of them up for not respecting such a beautiful old building but too many people about, can't risk it. Can't get up stairs without shoving people out of the way so we decide to take the polite route and wait very patiently and smile while the hundred people get from the top to the bottom of the stairs. It takes forever. An ignorant man behind us decides he can't wait for people coming down and starts to push in front of us. That is until Husband gives him a great death stare and he steps back. Where does he think he is going any way? He'd never get up the stairs with those big clown shoes on.

Every time we enter a room which already has people in they are pawing at the walls and Victorian features and then they start talking really quietly like it's a secret to us what they are saying. Sod them. We immediately start talking in loud voices about the damp in the corner and the floor boards that are slipping away around it. We get stared at quite a lot during this viewing. Ha ha ha. Can't help ourselves now. We immediately go to the next room which is another reception room and find fault with the windows which are rotting badly and how surprised we are that they haven't dropped out yet and how dangerous it could be. In the bedrooms we comment on how overlooked the house is. Oh and the buses will really shake and vibrate the house when they go past. Also how the school will be really loud, not just in the morning but all day. We also impart loudly with the information that we think the school has got some real problems. If you can't beat them, worry and upset them.

In the overgrown garden people are looking at the house pretending to know what they are looking at. We discuss the cracks in the stone work that we can just see beginning to appear.

Had enough of watching other people in our house and listening to their crap and go home to cut the grass.

Carpet man coming tomorrow to give them a clean, thought it would make house look brighter and cleaner for selling. It is cheaper than buying a new carpet. Move some small things in readiness. Husband has retired to his PlayStation so find myself doing this with the help of the dog and cat who tirelessly try to trip me up with my hands full. What fun! Scowl at Husband as he goes through the game killing loads of slow moving, moaning and dribbling zombies. Looks familiar. May have seen some of these zombies at the character house today.

Monday 11 February

Carpet man is here on time. Have shifted settee about, dining room furniture is in the kitchen and the half blind dog is on the garden so she doesn't bump into things because they are in a different place.

Carpet man is quite grumpy. Decide to stay out of his way. Besides, I am trapped in the kitchen with most of the downstairs furniture. The dog has had enough outside and scratches on back door. She is a persistent little git. Climb over cabinet to let her in before she digs her way in under the patio and walks over newly cleaned carpets. Have made about 34 cups of tea for grumpy man and Husband. Not getting biscuits out though. Don't want crumbs in newly cleaned carpets. If they want biscuits they will have to eat them over the sink or stand on the garden. Anyway, don't think grumpy carpet man deserves my nice Jammy Dodgers.

The cleaning seems to be taking ages. It wasn't that dirty was it? Hear a call from grumpy man to ask me to decide what smell I want spraying on the carpets to make them smell nice and not of the cleaning products. All of the sprays smell the same, it is so hard deciding. Call Husband down from his office upstairs to help. We decide on a flowery one just in case other people can tell the difference. Just as I thought, the spray doesn't hide the smell of the cleaning products at all; at least my nostrils are clear now.

Grumpy man drags all of his equipment back to the van. Before he takes it all he leaves a questionnaire to fill in about service etc and a spectacular fridge magnet, small notebook and the bill. Thanks

When grumpy man drives away in his van we realise he has dumped the dirty water down the grate on the road. Only it has run over the pavement as well. It is full of cat hair, dust and muck. This will look good for anyone doing a drive by. Thanks for that you twat.

I move all the furniture back to its home and we have a late dinner. The cat wants dinner as well. Feed her and she promptly returns the favour by bringing it all back up in the middle of the newly cleaned dining room carpet. Again, thanks for that.

Tuesday 12 February

See a property on-line which we have overlooked because of a main road at the bottom of the garden. Ring the agents to arrange a viewing. The vendor can make tonight. Great, don't have to wait. Brochure on-line doesn't give many pictures so I am quite intrigued to see the décor. It is probably dated if there is a lack of photos.

We arrive at 4.30pm on the dot after getting lost several times on the estate trying to find it. Good job we set off early.

Note to self
- take the Sat Nav on all future viewings

House is different. It is split level over 4 floors with great views out of the back. But oh my God. When the front door opened it was like walking into a pub taproom before the smoking ban had kicked in. We couldn't see anything through the thick smog. We called this house Smokey Jo's.

I was right about the décor. Typical of this estate, very, very dated. Owners seem to like it though. Hope they take carpets, curtains, kitchen and bathroom with them. House style was good but next door's driveway had about 7 cars on it. When we asked the vendor if she knew anything about them she said they were just a big family. Don't think so, looks like they are from a garage because as we drive off Husband notices same garage name on some of the cars. Decide this one isn't for us. Don't want cars revving up at all times of day with people turning up at the house for work to be done to their cars or to view potential new cars.

Have been thinking. Can you die from second hand smoke seeping out of the walls while you are sleeping?

Wednesday 13 February

The agents rang about the open viewing house on Sunday. They have had 5 offers in, we are in second place. Quite good. Having another open viewing on 17 February. Not so good. It is actually really crap. Very depressing.

Decide to view the James Bond bungalow again that needs the layout redesigning. Appointment is for 4pm tomorrow. Maybe Husband and I could live in a bungalow. We are now pushing 30 and nothing else is in the running really. Why not plan for our retirement now? Who needs stairs in a house anyway? They're not compulsory are they?

Ring a mortgage company about figures for the character house, just in case we manage to get it. Oh look, it's a flying pink piggy.

We could just manage to buy character house and keep ours to live in until the character house has a kitchen. Then we could sell present house to help fund renovations on character house. Just need to wait and see now if we get it.

Thursday 14 February

Other couples are getting ready for a night of delicious food, presents and passion. We have another house viewing. Yippee.

Same feelings for the James Bond house, or should I say bungalow, or maybe, one level living in the county?

It is on a good plot, but we feel it needs too much work doing to it for the price that is being asked. We have also heard it has previously been on the market before for about 2 years with another agent and didn't sell. The vendors were still weird and still followed us both everywhere.

We head to McDonalds for a Valentines burger and latte.

Watch TV. Is all that's on TV at the moment house shows? Give us a break! Not tonight darling, have a headache the size of a house.

Friday 15 February

Get a tip off regards a new property on the market. We have spies everywhere. A For Sale sign has been spotted. We ring the agents to make an appointment. Oh my God. It's another bungalow. It is two doors down from the one we viewed yesterday. They are in direct competition with each other.

An appointment has been made for tomorrow. At least we don't have to wait too long to see it, it's not even on-line yet.

Big plot ☺
Detached ☺
Next to a public footpath (used mainly by people stealing from the local farmer) ☹
Next to railway lines ☹

At least the other bungalow is further away from the footpath and railway lines, even though it has been beaten with the ugly stick, many a time over.

Saturday 16 February

Viewing bungalow next to railway and footpath this morning. The property has a good feeling about it inside but it still feels as dated as the other one two doors up but it is decorated more professionally.

It is on a good sized plot with views over your own paddock. The property is quite spacious inside. Oh my God! A kitchen that is actually nice and newish. Double garage, this pleases Husband. It has a room over the double garage which could be turned into an amazing PlayStation room apparently.

En-suite ☺
Cloaks ☺
Double garage ☺
Big garden ☺

It is ticking all dream wish list so far. It is not old and quaint with character though. It is also a bungalow. Oh well, can't have it all, or can you? I certainly want it. We decide this property needs considering. Perhaps it could be our one level living detached country residence. Sounds quite grand.

But then we remember the stories of local houses being broken into and the thieves using the footpath at the side of this property to escape with their swag bag. What to do …..

Sunday 17 February

Open viewing again on the character property. Drove past but didn't bother going in this time. Lots of cars parked all over again, most parked like twats. How many more open viewings are needed? The agents tell us that the church have to be seen achieving the best price possible. Ok then. Loads of people wandering round looking up at the roof and the around the garden pretending they know what they are looking for. The usual group of kids are running around the garden and appear to belong to no one.

Sad aren't I? Just downloaded Google Earth and now we can see all the properties we are interested in from the air. It's great for seeing the size of a plot and how close other houses are. You can also see if there is a railway line or footpath. Think I am addicted or mad.

Monday 18 February

Fed up of estate agents pushing mortgages instead of houses. Have to spend at least 5 minutes telling them we'll come and talk to their mortgage adviser when we want to offer on a property so we don't waste anyone's time (especially ours). Plus the figures will be more up to date when we actually find a house and then see a mortgage adviser.

Rang up our lovely mortgage people and complained to them, they said to tell the agents to ring them as we have already had our mortgage agreed on principal with them and it will stop the estate agents harassing us every time we ring to view a property. We know our limit and have an idea of monthly payments from the nice mortgage people.

Just need something to spend our money on now. I wonder where we will end up living, an old property, bungalow or a caravan?

Tuesday 19 February

Second viewing today at 10.30am on the detached one level country residence at the side of the railway and footpath. Husband and I are no clearer. We still like it but it still has the footpath and railway which won't be going away any time soon. Some axe murderer could come in the night, kill us both then escape down the footpath without anyone seeing. Apart from the neighbouring horses if they aren't asleep. Do horses sleep? Decisions, decisions.

Going back again the bedrooms seem smaller but the kitchen is still good. Driveway seems steeper than I remembered and the room above the garage feels very cold even though the sun is shining. Thought about changing the double garage into a dining room because it is off of the kitchen and utility room. We could build a new garage at the other side of the bungalow on the lower bit of the drive.

Thoughts of reading the Sunday newspapers in the beautiful kitchen of the detached one level country residence springs to mind with a coffee then we realise we wouldn't be able to afford to buy papers with a mortgage that big. We will also have to make our own coffee, probably using the hot water tap if the kettle breaks as we wouldn't be able to afford a replacement.

Husband rings the agents selling the lovely barn conversion. They still haven't got back to us regarding the part exchange. We also asked what sound proofing it had because it is attached on both sides. Would not want to hear the neighbours having sex through the walls as we do now in our semi at the moment. It sounds like a pig being slaughtered. We could spend loads of money buying the barn and still hear next door and their antics.

Wednesday 20 February

Have a viewing today for a new built house which is a few years old in our desired location. It is near to all of the doctor's surgery style houses but obviously it is cleaner, fresher and newer. Just what the doctor ordered.

It is an empty property so it is an accompanied viewing. We arrive a few minutes early and the agent showing us around is not here yet. There is a couple here with a uniformed girl fresh from school. They are parked on the driveway to the property. It is a wide double drive that narrows towards the road; they are parked at the end near the road so we can't pull on. Husband does though, he manages to squeeze on the end and we don't half get a stare from the woman. Can feel the daggers hitting the side of my head while we wait in the car. They should have parked considerately, where is the agent supposed to park? Twats.

It is freezing outside and they are stood on the porch as if they are waiting for a race to begin. We sit in the nice warm car and stare back at her. Her rather plump, downtrodden husband and uniformed child go back to their car to wait while she stays on the porch. She seems to be hanging on to the door handle as if her life depended on it. We decide to call her Squinty Num Num. We sat observing them from the car. A clear pecking order seems to be taking place, Squinty Num

Num then Gertrude the uniform and then her plump, downtrodden husband at the bottom.

While sitting in the car we notice a footpath opposite the house. The house looks lovely.

On a big plot ☺
Detached ☺
Big garden ☺
Double garage ☺
Wide driveway ☺

The agent turns up and Squinty Num Num races in the house before her family. When we get inside we take our shoes off and go upstairs after making pleasantries with the agent. They have gone into the kitchen.

It is a bit disappointing. Rooms don't feel that big, hallway seems to take over the upstairs. Downstairs there is a tiny dining room and lounge. The kitchen is nice with a small family area off it. Every time we stop to talk with the agent Squinty Num Num is hanging around craning her neck trying to listen. It doesn't help that we know the agent from other accompanied viewings and she seems jealous. Never mind, it's her problem.

The agent takes us around the garden to show us in the double garage. Squinty Num Num is very jealous and is staring at us through the windows while they are upstairs. She should have thought to ask to look in the garage. After looking in here we have seen enough and we leave. We do like this house.

Thursday 21 February

We go back to the newish house we viewed yesterday and park up. We follow the footpath that we spotted to find out where it goes. Oh my God! It's a shortcut to the main road. But oh my God! It is a teenage hangout on a massive scale. Beer cans, bottles, litter and chewing gum wrappers are everywhere! There are a few different bushy areas with trees that have been trashed with broken branches. The fence opposite the path has been set on fire a couple of times and further down the delightful children have knocked out or rather kicked the hell out of some panels. We decide this house is not for us, can't be this close to unruly teenagers.

Squinty Num Num is welcome to this house, wonder if they will become prisoners in their own home when the teenagers decide to widen their net of destruction.

It's a real shame about the location of this house because we both really liked it despite the small rooms.

Checked the lottery numbers for last night. Oh well, never mind. Will try again on Saturday. Why can't we win the lottery? Only a couple of hundred thousand would be great, we're not greedy.

Friday 22 February

Agent rings regards the house near the teenager den of destruction. Tell her it's not for us. I tell her about the teenager hangout and she says, 'when you're spending a lot of money you want it to be right.'

Too true Mrs.

Spent all morning trying to make appointments to view 3 properties for tomorrow. Oh my God, this is hard work. How this could be done if I had a real job beggars belief!

It felt good telling the agents that we have got a mortgage sorted. Saved at least half an hour on the phone.

Decided to look at houses slighter cheaper than we had originally planned. It would reduce the mortgage and stress.

Bought supermarkets own brand hairspray today to save some money. Oh my God! Was like spraying fresh air onto my hair. Waste of 37p. Could have gone towards next latte or lottery ticket.

False economy doesn't work. As my uncle says, 'buy cheap buy twice.' Spot on uncle.

Saturday 23 February

Fingers crossed; will we be lottery millionaires tonight? Probably not. Some criminal somewhere will be instead.

Two viewings today and one tomorrow. The first house has got the old features we want, it is double fronted but parking is nowhere near as the house is up a hillside. Also, there are public footpaths surrounding the house.

House is lovely inside, full of Victorian features but just not suitable for us. We really need the parking as the side of the house not half a mile down the road.

The next viewing is a new house on a small development. Beautiful house from the outside and a much nicer sales negotiator on site. Not a snobby bitch at all. Layout spacious downstairs, but as we reach the first floor the rooms are decidedly smaller. Where would our wardrobes fit? Think the house would be better suited as a 3 bed not 4 beds. The builder has squeezed too many rooms upstairs. It would suit a hamster looking for a challenging new maze not a couple with loads of crap.

We take the information pack anyway because we like the site. The thing to think about is if we can live in the house or it if is too small.

Sunday 24 February

Another new house viewing today. It was supposed to have been yesterday. It was hard booking the appointment at the time, the agents weren't very helpful then they rang up yesterday afternoon and asked if it could be today because the lady showing us around was having car trouble. They knew when I rang to make the appointment yesterday that they would cancel. Do they want to sell houses or not?

It is a small development of 4 houses. It is a beautiful house on 3 floors although the kitchen is smaller than I want but all of the other rooms are large. There are countryside views out of the front windows, that is until the builder has planning permission to build on the land in front of this house.

The back garden has stone steps up to it with fruit trees planted in the grass. Quite nice but the half blind dog will need carrying up and down the steps. Oh my God. The garden backs onto a pub car park and beer garden. Great. Lots of car noise and children screaming all summer, sorry, children having fun. The pub is also empty at the moment and is up for letting, you could get any sort of pub opening back up. Keep looking maybe?

Wonder if we can hire a big crane to lift this house and put it on the house we are going to be selling.

Monday 25 February

We are still waiting to hear back on our offer for the character property being sold by the church. This is taking ages.

Have a chat with Husband and are both fed up. We decide to offer on the detached abode in the country that we first viewed weeks ago. It is the bungalow which is not next to the railway or footpath, the one that Husband thinks is like a James Bond house.

Ring the agents up and put the offer in, start the long wait now for our offer to be rejected. At least all of the agents calling for feedback on viewed properties keeps me busy through the day.

Note to self
- check lottery numbers.

Agents call back this afternoon regards the bungalow offer. It has been rejected. Too low. Decide not to offer again just yet, let them wait. There are 3 other properties for sale in the same road. It won't be selling that fast. Will offer again when the character property with the church is done with. The closing day for offers on that property is tomorrow. Have a feeling that we won't get it. A builder who has loads of cash to throw at it probably will. We will then drive past it all finished and think why didn't we get that?

Tuesday 26 February

The closing day is today. All offers to be in by 12 noon. I ring mid-morning so I don't appear too eager. Our second offer is now in. Have to wait now, could know this afternoon or in a few days. I clean the house and potter in the garden. Look at some magazines. Decide to move the lounge furniture around for a change. Husband won't notice for a few days then I will change it back. He thinks I'm messing with his mind when I do this and he actually notices.

Had phone calls from agents regards some viewings. It is hard not to be too critical about properties but someone is going to be rude about ours when we have viewings. Don't feel too bad.

Wednesday 27 February

Still haven't heard anything about our offer on the character property, presume we have not been successful. Need to keep looking but there is nothing new on the market. How come there seems to be more than a fair share of dated bungalows in our area?

The agents dealing with the barn conversion rang this afternoon. They said the builder would consider a part exchange and she will get back to us.

Didn't win the lottery. Crap.

Search the internet and find a property new to the market on the doctor's surgery style house estate. It is a bungalow, again. But it is on a big plot with a massive garage for Husband to play in. Ring to make an appointment. Vendor can make tonight.

Only got lost once around the estate this time. Once we had worked our way around the estate maze we parked on the drive and walked up to the door weaving around several cars. As soon as we rang the bell the door was yanked open and the questioning began.

Woman in her 50's with dark mad hair stood staring down at us. She was supposed to own a clothes shop, boutique thing, but she obviously didn't wear what she sold in there, unless she sold flowery sacks.

64

The questioning went like this:

'Have you had a promotion?' – Checking we could afford the property.

'Have you got children?' – Don't know what this had to do with the viewing.

'Where do you live now?'

'I have had a cash offer already, are you offering cash?' – Is she crazy?

'When can you move in?' – When ours is sold.

She moved us quickly through the property which had fake pillars and coving everywhere. It was decorated like a plaster of Paris shop. When the crazy lady opened the garage door it was literally full of crap from floor to ceiling. Apparently it all belonged to her sons who had moved out years ago and not yet sorted it out. Most of the cars parked on the drive were also her sons who had left them there. There must have been 4 cars that weren't hers.

We didn't hang around long as we didn't want the lie detector machine hooking up. She would see through our lies why we didn't want to buy it. Made our excuses and left as soon as crazy woman stopped to draw breath. A viewing has never been so tiring.

Stop off for extra strong coffee on the way home.

Thursday 28 February

In the post today was a letter confirming the offer we placed on the character church property. We still haven't been notified if we are successful or not. That's estate agents for you.

Try to make a booking for a house viewing on Sunday. The agents ring the vendor and then come back to us. They can't make Sunday as she is going out to lunch. It doesn't take all day to eat does it? Agents call back to say she could make today or tomorrow. Husband working, will have to be next weekend.

The agents selling the character church property ring at lunchtime to let us down. We didn't get the highest bid and have lost the property. Thought we would but strangely we both feel very relieved.

Tick it off and move on.

It saves us being woken up in term time by a crazy school run with 4x4 vehicles and screaming kids.

Friday 29 February

The agents dealing with the James Bond bungalow we offered on rang today. She asked, 'Have you considered raising your offer?'

Have the vendors considered not being greedy and reducing their price? This is the burning question.

Do they realise how dated their house is? Maybe they need to go and get checked for glasses instead of relying on the telescope all of the time.

March

Get cleaning

Clean, hoover and dust everywhere! If you stay on top of the cleaning the weekly routine won't be such a big job when you do have viewers look around your house. This includes windows and mirrors.

Saturday 1 March

We have an appointment to view another house on the doctor's surgery estate. It is booked in for 10.30am. We arrive about 10.20am and decide to wait in the car for 5 minutes or so before knocking on the door. We were just looking through housing section in local paper we had picked up on the way when there was a tap on the window.

It was an old lady. Here we go. Are we parked wrong? Are we dressed wrong for the area? Are we parked in her spot?

Turns out it is the woman from the house we are looking at. 'Are you here to look at the house?' she asks.

'Yes, we have an appointment at 10.30am.'

'Oh,' she says. 'I have an appointment at the hairdressers in 10 minutes. I told the agents it wasn't a good time.'

Husband and I look at each other and roll our eyes.

'I suppose my husband can show you around,' she says as she walks off in a cloud of old lady perfume waving her hand in the air for us to follow even before we had the chance to tell her we will ring the agents.

We get to the doorstep and she appears again. To say she is supposed to be at the hairdressers soon she finds time to quickly show us around the downstairs rooms. Her husband says, 'you'd better be going or you'll be late.' This gets rid of her but before she goes she tells us that if we talk to her husband we will have to 'shout at him'. She turns to her husband and says, 'they've got to shout at you haven't they?' He just nods his head. Oh dear, poor sod. Why has he not strangled her to death yet?

She disappears in a puff her foul perfume and we continue the tour around. We are not keen on the layout but even though the house is dated it is clean and liveable. We chat with the deaf man but find we don't have to shout, he can understand us easily in our normal voices. We get to the kitchen which appears to be the workmanship hub of the house. Bless him. The old man shows us every cupboard, nook and cranny very proudly. Apparently he helped choose all the special features like a pull out ironing board etc. He was very proud.

In the end we thanked him without shouting and politely left. Another house that is not for us. Another mistake from the agents.

Sunday 2 March

Sod this for a game of house hunting. We decide to go for a drive in the countryside; it is a beautiful sunny day. Sod houses. I make up a flask of coffee and raid the cake tin. Now we're ready.

Discover a new house site while out driving. We spotted the strategically placed little yellow signs on lampposts and obediently followed them. The site is not too big with beautiful houses with a mix and 2 and 3 floors and L shaped designs which we love. The houses are in the middle of nowhere so there is a shocking lack of amenities, how do the locals survive? Because it is in the middle of nowhere the site does have beautiful countryside with sheep in fields near to the houses. The builders have also left some mature trees dotted around the estate instead of cutting them all down.

We have arrived about 5 minutes before the open sign says but someone is inside the office. We decide to go in. Big mistake. 'We're not open yet,' spits the sales negotiator with last night's garlic on her breath. 'Sorry we thought you were, the door was open,' I said. 'No,' she replies. Husband and I give each other the familiar look when she then says, 'I suppose you could look at the show house while I make my coffee.' Oh thank you kind garlic lady, we are honoured. Maybe a truck load of strong mints wouldn't go a miss either while you're in the kitchen.

The negotiator may have a customer who is about to spend over £¼ million with them and treats them like that, typical.

We look round the show house and I start doing that stroking thing again with the soft furnishings. Husband just looks at me and disappears. He has again disappeared in the quest of finding a suitable PlayStation room.

We do like the houses but we're not sure of the sites location. We take the house information get in the car and carry on with our drive. We start looking for a lay by with a view to stopping and devouring our cakes and coffee.

If this site was closer to the motorway for access and had some local shops it could be a goer. We haven't yet dismissed it though after mentally going through our dream house check list because a couple of the house styles match our list.

Monday 3 March

Mobile ringing but vacuuming and didn't hear it. Got a message left and then the house phone rang. It's an agent asking about the viewing we missed on Saturday!

Oh my God. We didn't have a call to say a viewing had been arranged for us. Apparently it was the property of the woman who was having the large lunch all day on Sunday.

Anyway, agent's uselessness overcome, viewing arranged properly for Saturday at 11.30am. Also a viewing for the new property with the pub in the back garden at 10am on Saturday. This viewing is to finally decide if we want it or not, or in other words if we want to become alcoholics or not.

I finish doing the hovering and go to the shops. I leave my mobile phone at home. Can't think straight. Need to purchase something. Need to buy quickly.

Friday 7 March

Lovely Mortgage Company rang today to see if we had found a property and if we needed any more figures.

It was ages ago that I rang them and we still haven't got anything yet. Oh my God. Is it me or do other people do this much quicker than us?

The agent rang today about the James Bond bungalow we had offered on. No, we are not going to increase offer, not on your nelly. The vendors won't budge below the asking price anyway so they're stuffed. They have also not had any viewings or offers since ours.

Note to self
- buy the local paper and feed the dog.

Saturday 8 March

We have two viewings today. Really don't feel inspired. Husband and I just couldn't see ourselves living in these houses.

What is up with us?
Wrong house type?
Wrong price bracket?
Wrong area?

This is a puzzler!

Pub car park versus decoration from hell – which to choose?

Neither are desirable houses. Sod them all. Go to McDonalds for a chewing burger and latte.

Sunday 9 March

There is nothing on the horizon. We can't decide where to buy or what to buy. There is nothing on the telly and the neighbours were having sex again last night. Could hear them through the walls like they were putting on a show as if to say, 'yep, we are old but we can still have sex.' We could camp on the garden but she is that loud we would probably hear her out there as well.

Wednesday 19 March

A change in the economy is happening. Crap.

Fed up with house hunting and we still haven't got ours on the market yet. Still can't decide whether to find something first then sell ours or sell ours and then look for something. It hasn't helped looking at new properties with part exchanges on them.

We decide to go away over the Easter weekend. Pick Devon. Lovely. Husband books tomorrow off work and I start packing. Too much thinking really does hurt and confuse the mind.

I spend the rest of the day finding a hotel and places to visit while we are there. Mustn't forget to book a surfing lesson for Husband.

Thursday 20 March

Leave our lovely neighbours the keys, the cat and the half blind dog, which happens to have started her season and we set off at break next speed. Damn dog. We are back home Saturday evening anyway.

Journey not too bad. All the beautiful coastal villages and countryside gets us thinking. Why not move to Devon?

We can't find anything interesting or desirable in our locality back home.

Get to Devon and check into the hotel. First things first and we set off to the beach. Maybe get some fish and chips on the way. Lovely.

Friday 21 March

Spotted some new house site signs while driving and decide to have a look at them and collect some information. The sales staff seem thoroughly miserable. Don't they like tourists? We soon win them over with our Yorkshire flair, wit and sense of humour. We have already learnt that you need sales negotiators and agents on your side.

We look around the show home with a negotiator and continue laying on the Yorkshire charm. Nice size house for the money. Kind lady shows us the site plans and where these houses are on the site. We walk round with her to look at the 3 of them that we like.

The house we like is on a corner and has 4 bedrooms, dining room, kitchen diner, en-suite and a valley at the end of the large garden. No one overlooking the garden and the back of the house but other houses at the front will be able to see what we are watching on TV and what we eat for breakfast.

This could be really good though. Prices are much cheaper than we thought they would be for the area.

Head back to the hotel for a rest after using too much energy being witty and nice. It is very tiring being charming.

Oh, by the way, Devon is beautiful by the time we eventually get around to seeing the sites. Lovely beaches. Maybe we could buy a tent and live on the beach. We could become surfer dudes. Wonder what the cat would think though. Seagulls might eat her. Although the beach would be a gigantic litter tray for her.

We find a pub for something to eat and decide to stay in there for the evening.

Saturday 22 March

Head back to the new house site and look around again. Drive around the local area and find the doctors and dentists. Also stumble across a supermarket.

Note to self
- don't go to seaside supermarket on a Saturday, too full of tourists

Go back to beach and have fish and chips. Do other holiday stuff, i.e. buy useless tat. Although do discover a nice little shop full of delicious home wares and trinkets. I love it, Husband waits outside. While outside he notices a coffee/bistro which he takes me to and buys me a coffee and a bun. Lovely. What a thoroughly thoughtful person he is.

Tuesday 25 March

Back home. Husband and I still think Devon could be the place for us. For once we are quite excited about the houses there, what does that say?

Start planning another weekend away to view houses and areas again.

Book Premier Inn in Barnstaple, cheaper than last hotel. Do some research on-line. Have found two areas, one town close to the beach and one overlooking a beach. Need to research areas now.

Realise though that these areas have a vastly reduced lack of shops, supermarkets etc. And would those that existed be really busy? Would supermarkets do home delivery? Need to check postcodes.

Have discovered Croyde! Looks ace! Oh my God! Have you seen the house prices there? Far too expensive for us, more of a place to visit. Let's leave it at that.

Thursday 27 March

Our next excursion to Devon is all sorted, can't wait to go now.

I was expecting a house back on the market this week which was previously being rented out but is now being sold as the tenants have moved out. The agents called to say this property is not available to view for another 2 months now. That's a shame; it is a nice old property with 3 bedrooms and masses of character. We will just have to wait a bit longer.

Friday 28 March

Pack today, we are driving down to Devon at teatime to arrive evening time.

Leave the keys, dog (still in season) and cat again with lovely neighbours and set off.

Note to self
- need to get the neighbours a good present

Arrive about 11pm ish feeling very tired. Doubts start creeping in. Are we making a huge mistake? Weather is dull and raining. It is like gloom juice falling.

We check in to the hotel and lovely girl on reception tell us that the Chuckle Brothers are staying here as well. They are performing in Barnstaple this weekend. Husband is really impressed, me not so much.

We lug our bags up to room; apparently I have packed too much stuff, and make a coffee. Husband wonders if we will be able to hear Chuckle Brothers moving furniture around their room saying, 'to me, to you, to me, to you.'

I fall asleep while Husband is still listening at the door for furniture being shifted about.

Saturday 29 March

Wake up feeling a bit more optimistic. Have breakfast and head out to new house site we found at the Easter weekend. We have an appointment at 10am to look at the corner house again.

Love the house! Cheap, detached, double garage, big garden and bushy valley. What can we do to move as quickly as we can?

Drive out to Westward Ho! Because we love the name and wonder what is there. Would we find cowboys? All of a sudden the Cath Kidston catalogue springs to mind and I think about a lovely cowboy bag that I have seen…..

Fall in love with a new house site here as well as Bideford. This is a smaller site, slightly more expensive but closer to a beach but still with no sea view. The houses are all detached with 4 bedrooms and are all large inside.

Decisions, decisions……

Negotiator on this site says they could be willing to do a part exchange with us. How exciting, it would make for an easy move. We leave our details to start things rolling.

We head off to Woolacombe; we already know this area and know we can only afford to stay here in a hotel for a week, or to live on the side of the road in a camper van. It could be fun.

Find a bistro attached to the nice hotel we have stayed at which is new since we last visited. Find a seat overlooking the sea and order loads of food.

Maybe we could sell our house and then live in the hotel with the money from the sale. Nope, wouldn't work because cat wouldn't be prepared with work as a hotel rat catcher. She would be far too lazy and would prefer to lay down being fed kitty treats and milk.

Sunday 30 March

Have breakfast. Still haven't seen the Chuckle Brothers around the hotel. Husband very disappointed.

We had a drive last night through both areas we like and discussed while eating breakfast.

Sun shining but feel a little bit home sick, fears are creeping in now. Would it be better as a holiday location rather than living here permanently? After speaking to friends and family I think they are thinking we would be a cheap holiday destination.

Pack up and do some more holiday stuff. We have a look at Croyde. It's a brilliant place to visit but too expensive for us to live there.

Drive home.

Back home with the local paper after picking it up on way in. New house site 10 miles away. We are tired but decide to go and have a look. We both love the site.

Oh my God. Why does this have to be so hard? There seems either too much or too little to choose from.

April

Get minor repairs or small jobs done

All those jobs that you have been putting off need to be done. Touch up and replace anything broken as your buyer will only try to knock down the asking price if they have to do them.

Monday 7 April

The house site in Bideford rings. She will check to see if they could do a part exchange if the other builder is. She calls back later and yes they can do a part exchange. Amazing, it wasn't an option when we were actually on site.

She agrees to try. She says that some local agents will contact us to arrange a valuation of our property.

I ring a removal company for a quote to move us to Devon. They are coming on Thursday.

I start tidying and chucking clutter. Why have we got so much crap? Even the charity shop won't take it all.

Wednesday 9 April

I clean the house even though it is only the removal man coming for a valuation tomorrow. I hope this isn't becoming a habit. I don't want visitors expecting a clean house every time they call.

The phone rings and it is an agent wanting to come round to value the house for the part exchange. I make the appointment for tomorrow afternoon after the removal company has been and quoted. At least the house will still look presentable for them.

Thursday 10 April

The removal company is in this morning to quote. Agent for valuation is this afternoon for the part exchange.

Not heard from the site yet in Westward Ho! regards the valuations. We set her off with the task before the other one at Bideford. Another useless person in the quest of trying to sell houses.

I need to mop kitchen floor, the dog hinders this small job by getting in the way trying to hump the cat and my leg and the mop bucket. Water goes everywhere. Crap, I now need lots of towels for a mop up job the actual mop isn't doing a good job.

Note to self
-    give the negotiator at Westward Ho! a call to get things moving

The removal man turns up on time. He is very round and jolly and is instantly likeable. He reminds me of Father Christmas. Although he does say we have a lot of stuff. Husband just stares at me. I know this look; it means I have a lot of stuff. He tells us he should be able to post the quote tonight for tomorrow morning. That's good service.

The valuer turns up this afternoon for the part exchange valuation. There is something about him that makes me think,'tosser.' He has a quick look around the house and then promptly leaves while saying anything apart from the builder will contact us regards the part exchange price, on his way out of the door.

Wednesday 16 April

A new property has come to the market on the doctor's surgery estate and it isn't a bungalow! Whoopee!

It ticks most boxes; it's on a corner plot so the garden is quite big and it is a 4 bed with ensuite.. Ring up for a viewing; they can do this evening at 6.30pm.

House had a good feeling, a little tired in décor with dated wallpaper on most walls but it could work. Most of the furniture looked like it was from a photo shoot from the Next catalogue. The house had a single garage, but with an electric door. Husband ok with that. It has a beer fridge in the kitchen! Although it has a huge private conifer hedge surrounding the plot you can't see much over it. Most houses on this estate seem to have huge conifer hedges, are they not very friendly with each other?

The lady showing us around was quite small. She was ok but got the feeling that she didn't like us. Her haircut reminded us of a 12 year old. It was a short bob with a fringe. We made polite conversation during the viewing but left feeling disliked. We decide to call her Child haircut but we liked her house.

Thursday 17 April

Really liked the house last night, have rung the agents to make an appointment to view it again. Going on Sunday at 10am, it was made earlier because we have got to be back in time for the Formula one race, Husband says.

Note to self
- check lottery numbers from last night

Had a phone call this afternoon from the agents who are selling the character property for the church. The winning bid has fallen through and they were ringing to see if we were still interested. Told them no thanks. Not getting into that again. If our offer and position to move wasn't good enough first place, sod them. And besides, we have really gone off houses with foot paths along the side of them. It's asking for trouble or in other words, kids drinking beer and stealing along with unwelcome noises.

Saturday 19 April

We are working in the garden today keeping it looking something like for when we go to market. Get grass cut and trim some bushes. Garage still needs tidying up as it appears to have accumulated more crap since the last time we were in there. It must be the cat or the dog bringing things back with them when they go out.

Get local paper and check housing section. Nothing new in for us. Waste of money. Again. Even though we look on line you may spot something else in the paper which keeps us buying it. Besides, we save old copies for an old uncle who likes to go through the obituaries to update his address book.

Sunday 20 April

It is warm but drizzly today. The house on the corner still looks good. They have had no interest since we looked on Wednesday. Good for us. It feels a little smaller today but still very liveable. It has 4 beds, en-suite, utility, study and dining room. Child Haircut is a bit nicer to us today. Probably because she thinks we may buy the house because of the second viewing.

We are back in time for Formula 1. Husband is happy.

Have a drive around at teatime and find a new board up in a little village we like. Need to arrange a viewing.

Note to self
- ring agents to try and make an appointment to view property which is new to the market

Monday 21 April

Ring the agents to arrange a viewing on the new to the market village property. Oh my God! How hard can it be to arrange a time and date?

The vendor is letting the agents do accompanied viewings on her property but she is insisting that she be there as well. The vendor's husband has just gone into hospital. Phone calls and conversations fly about and we finally arrange to view on 24th April at 5pm.

We know already that the interior will be very dated if an elderly couple live there but it has the location in its favour. We are prepared for hard work, muck and lots of expense.

It is a detached house with a double garage in a predominately bungalow area again. What a result.

Thursday 24 April

Viewing for the hard to make appointment property today at 5pm. It takes forever to get to 4.45pm when we set off. Use Google Earth to see size of the plot etc. It looks ok; fields are behind the house it will be nice and quiet. It is not near a footpath but trains pass through at the end of the road.

House very dated as we thought. Layout is ok but massive stone fire place in the living room. Lovely. House feels generally small inside with no proper back door. You would have to go through the kitchen then the utility room and then the garage to get on the back garden. Agent showing us around recognises us again which makes it easier looking around. Vendor who is an old lady sits on the settee not smiling the whole time we are viewing. We decide to call her Old Grumpy. The garden is big enough but not enclosed so will cost a bit to secure with fencing or the like to keep the disabled dog safe. The half blind cat would love to play in the fields at the back of the house. Just thought, would a tractor drive over her while she was snoozing in the field?

We are very interested in this property but we feel that the amount of work that needs doing the asking price is too steep.

List of jobs to update the house

- new electricals/rewiring
- new boiler
- new kitchen
- new cloaks
- replaster all walls (all walls are covered with old painted over wallpapers)

Friday 25 April

Get the local paper with the housing section in. The house on the corner plot is having an open day on Sunday. We decide we will go along and see if anyone else is looking. Still like this house even though some updating is needed.

The house builder in Devon calls today with a part exchange figure. We think it is slightly low and say we will get back to her. We are having doubts about moving this far away from what we are used to. Besides the quote from the removal company says it will cost a couple of grand to move all of our crap down there. We are feeling a bit chicken and want to back out because it feels too much at the moment to move so far away.

Note to self
- call the builder in Westward Ho!

Saturday 26 April

Go out for the morning to the local park for a walk and some exercise.

The second builder in Devon rings about the part exchange but there seems to be a problem which they haven't let us know about until now. The original sales negotiator was going on holiday which we knew about, but a wittering twit has replaced her. Husband tells her everything again. Then she calls back and says the builder is not prepared to do the part exchange now. How long has it taken to come to that conclusion? This site was our preferred one in Devon as well, feel deflated even though we were having doubts about this location.

Abandon our walk and call for a latte and muffin on the way home.

Note to self
- remember to check lottery numbers

Sun 27 April

Remembered to check the lottery numbers, ticket ran out last week.

Note to self
- remember to buy new ticket.

Open house is today on the corner plot. Turn up about 11am and no one else is there. Child Haircut has made a real effort, bless her; there are nibbles and drinks neatly arranged on the kitchen table and a basket with blue shoe cover things like in a show home.

She tells us that they are considering renting if the house doesn't sell soon because they have already bought another house.

We have another look around and still like it, don't think we could afford to buy and rent ours out.

Looks like we will miss this house because ours isn't even on the market yet. Crap. It may be the only nice house on the doctor's surgery estate that we like and isn't a bungalow.

Monday 28 April

Ring back the house builder in Devon. We have thought long and hard about this. Despite being in Devon and having a brand new house it just seems too much at the moment to make a move to Devon. Plus the job Husband was considering is not as it first seemed. We tell her thanks very much for all of her help but no thanks. We'll let her know if anything changes. Damn.

It was good while it lasted. It feels more like a holiday location for now. But we will have to move there in a few years so we can be surfer dudes and grow our hair long. Well, mine and the dog's really.

Decide we can make the most of our Lake District visits while we are closer to it. One of our favourite destinations for the day is Lake Windermere. We can be there in a few hours. Oh, and do some shopping at Lakeland while we are there. ☺

May

Kerb appeal

To attract buyers your house has got to look good
from the outside as well as sparkling on the inside.
Remember buyers do drive-bys to assess whether
or not it is worth even making an appointment to
view. Ensure grass is cut regularly in summer,
daises are pretty but don't sell houses and no one
wants to sit in a jungle.

Thursday 1 May

Rang the estate agents who came to value our property at the beginning of the year and check if the figures they provided are the same. They are the same; the agents don't need to come back out. Can't believe it was over 4 months ago. Doesn't time go by fast when you are stressed, tired and having no fun at all? Right this is it. We are going to market.

Ring the agent that kept being late to give them another chance. Now the housing market has taken a turn for the worst we thought 3 valuations would be better than 2. The appointment is for 6 May at 11am if they bother to turn up on time or at all! Looking forwards so much to their visit.

Sunday 4 May

In the garden today, Husband cut the grass and I tidied so it looks good for any external photographs the agents will take for the house brochure.

Bath the dog, she smells much better. She was much cleaner as well until she decided to dig up the heather flower bed on the patio and roll in the mess. This is her favourite spot in the garden, may have to pave over it. Bathed the dog again. She looked disgusted that I had interfered in her fun and designer doggy hair style.

Husband swept the patio and tried to re-plant the heathers without them looking odd or dead. Wonder how long we will have to wait for them to die. I will give them a week. It would be cheaper to pave over than keep refilling with plants.

Monday 5 May

Clean the house from top to bottom today in preparation for the valuation tomorrow. Now the inside looks as good as the outside. If the agents don't turn up tomorrow at least it looks good and is clean for us, but I may go round to their offices and throttle them.

Make a coffee, doesn't taste as good as a shop bought one, decide to put a dollop of squirty cream on top, much better. Cat is hanging around for some cream. She seems to know when any dairy product comes out of the fridge. Put a squirt of cream on my finger for her to lick off. The dog then decides she is being left out and all of a sudden is interested so she sticks her nose in the cat's cream. Doesn't like it and shakes it off. It lands on the floor where the cat dives on it and cleans it up. It saves mopping up at least.

Tuesday 6 May

Valuation today, agents are a little bit late ….

Twats.

Had a chat with him when he finally arrived, he seems to be ok and helped us with guidance and phrases to use when offering on properties. We decide to give them the benefit of the doubt and go to market with them. We have used them before, but the sale fell through. The staff have changed since last time. We get talking about films and movies and recommend some for him to watch. He runs out of time for signing paperwork and asks if he can come back after lunch to finish off and take photographs of the house.

I ring some solicitors for their charges and decide on one which is located at the top of our road, it has easy free parking.

The agent comes back to take the house pictures. Make sure the cat and dog weren't on the photos as they are not included in the fixtures and fittings. They would probably put prospective buyers off anyway.

End of the day,

Solictors found ☺
Paperwork signed ☺
Photos taken ☺

The For Sale board will go up outside in next couple of days.

The solicitors will post some forms for us to fill in.

It's all started now. We are not backing out. We will move from this house or die trying, hopefully this year.

Thursday 8 May

Filled forms in from the solicitors yesterday, taking them up to their office today. It is quicker than posting them. Need to take them a cheque as well because they are doing the HIPs pack for us. They are slightly cheaper than the estate agents. That will be money well spent because the HIPs pack is so important and worth every penny. Not.

The For Sale board goes up today. I keep looking out of the window for the van that puts them up to arrive. The Board Man is magical. He seems to be able to erect a for sale board without anyone seeing him.

Getting excited now. Just need to sit back and wait for the hundreds of viewers to come and look round. We could just be moving this year!

Note to self
- need to tell the neighbours that a for sale board will be going up before they see it for themselves

Friday 9 May

Solicitors sent the HIPs man out today to check the property at 10am. At least the house doesn't need cleaning for him. He was a pleasant chap but small. He had an even smaller set of ladders. I thought about saying something like, 'I know you're short but what are they for?' and offering him the loan of a larger set to use when I realised his ladders extended. He went around the house making notes and sticking his head in various places. Then he went outside to look at the exterior of the house.. He informed me he had finished and said that the solicitors would have the notes today and he then promptly left.

The draft brochure was sent out to us today. We need to check it for mistakes etc and send it back to the estate agents. Not too many mistakes, damn the house looks good, would buy it ourselves if we didn't own it already.

No appointments for viewers yet. Where are they all?

Saturday 10 May

Checked the draft brochure over and took it in to the estate agent's office so we can meet the staff that are selling our house. We also needed to take in some ID. Damn. I have tidied up too well, I can't find any.

End up rummaging through several drawers and cupboards around the house and stumble across the ID when looking for some toilet roll.

In the estate agent's office we chat with the agents and decide that it would be useful if one of the negotiators selling the house for us comes out to look at it. She will have a better idea when talking to prospective buyers about it and can push it better.

Appointment is booked in for Tuesday at 10am. Leave the agents feeling quite pleased.

Monday 12 May

Husband cut grass again yesterday.

I am cleaning house today so it looks the best it can when negotiator comes to look tomorrow.

Need a sit down. Make a coffee, quite like the squirty cream and put some on my coffee then I decide to cut out the middle man and squirt straight into mouth. Nice. The cat stares at me with a deadly look, glad I'm not a mouse or a rabbit. If she has too much cream she gets the trots and we can't have that now we have had the carpets cleaned. I turn my back to the cat so she can't see me but I can still feel her eyes burning into me.

Tuesday 13 May

The negotiator is due today at 10am. House is looking good. She is due any time now. It is now 10.15am, still waiting. Think they are always late will give them until 10.30am.

Ring the agents at 10.30am to find out where she is. She answers the phone. She was in a meeting which ran late and forgot she was coming. Ok. Translated, she couldn't be bothered as there wasn't a lift. She would have to catch the bus.

I re-arrange for tomorrow. 10am again. Oh my god. What a good start. Have we chosen the right estate agents? They seem to be turning into the agents from hell already.

Wednesday 14 May

Looking on-line at houses. A house new to the market has been found. Ring the agents to make an appointment to view. We are looking tonight at 7.30pm. It is on the estate we are looking at and is a house not a bungalow. Can't wait.

Negotiator turns up with the valuer. She turns up a very frilly, lacy blouse, with make-up put on with a trowel. Decide to call her Doily. She has a look around while the valuer tells me about some changes. Because of the credit crunch, the local estate agents have gotten together and decided not to advertise every week in the local paper. It will be every 3 weeks now. He also said that people weren't looking in the paper anymore and using the internet instead. Not true. We buy the paper. Doily had a quick look around and appears while the valuer is still talking.

All of a sudden they have to get going because they are late for another appointment. Maybe if they allow more time for each appointment then they wouldn't always be so late. I wonder if she needs frisking before she leaves, has she taken the crown jewels with her?

Tuesday 20 May

Our estate agents call today. They have someone wanting to view. At last! Yippee! An appointment is made for Thursday at 6pm.

Note to self
- wash dog's blanket
- keep the cat away from any dairy products to prevent the trots occurring

Wednesday 21 May

Spend the day cleaning and tidying. Because I have done this so many times now I have a set routine and can do it in about 2 hours. Anything that is still gets dusted so the cat and dog head outside to the garden whey they see the cleaning equipment being dragged out of the cupboards.

Apparently the viewing for tomorrow is a first time buyer. No chain. Hope they like it. We can move out quick if the occasion occurs. We have a tent.

Thursday 22 May

Takes all day to get to 6pm. Fill the time by reading magazines. I nip to the shops and I buy a few bits and a pineapple. Think it will improve the look of my fruit bowl. Probably will make us seem healthy, selling a lifestyle, that sort of thing.

The viewer is on her own but turns up on time. She says all the right things, loves the house, just right, just what she is looking for. Has to rush off though because she has got other houses to view. She took about 10 minutes to get around the house and the garden. Surely she missed something. I thrust a brochure into her hand as she leaves. Now need to sit back and wait for the agents to call with feedback or fingers crossed on an offer turning up.

Monday 26 May

Still no call from the agents with feedback from the viewing. Call them first. The viewer hasn't been contacted yet; they will call and let us know her response. Surely they should have been called by now. We usually have been when we've viewed a property.

Afternoon now and still no call. Will need to keep bugging the agents I suspect. I was right. We have the agents from hell working for us. We will probably never move house at all with these people involved.

Tuesday 27 May

Agents call with another viewer wanting to make an appointment for today. Then they change their minds and it is now on Thursday at 6pm. It's a good job we are nice people and can change appointments at the drop of a hat.

I mention feedback from the first viewer, they say they have been contacted now and the house is not for them. That's all they say, no more reasons or explanations.

I wish people wouldn't say they liked it if they don't really.

Thursday 29 May

I clean the house today in preparation for viewing later. Only trouble with these 6pm viewings is that tea is late. Always hungry at that time of the day.

The viewers turn up on time. A couple with a young girl. Turns out we have friends/work colleagues in common. We show them around the house trying to be really friendly, all the time thinking, when are you going to leave? We end up standing on the driveway talking for about half an hour after they have looked round the house. They don't seem to want to leave. All the time I am wondering if the neighbours are crouched behind the fence listening to everything we say. The viewers like the big garden and are raving about it. Well, as much as someone can rave who are so lack lustre and winy and pathetic looking.

Oh my god. Leave. Now.

Eventually they go and I rush into the kitchen to put a curry in the microwave for tea.

Saturday 31 May

Turns out the viewers from Thursday didn't like the house because it didn't have any high skirting boards, coving etc. They wanted a house with character.

Well you wouldn't find much of that in a 1960s semi would you. Didn't they look at the pictures at all? What a waste of time. Twats. All that time they kept us talking on the drive.

Feel really fed up now. Go for a latte and a donut.

The mobile phone rings while we are out in the car. It is the agents again with another viewer. This is a lady who is renting at the moment so isn't in a chain. An appointment made for Monday at 1pm.

Things are looking up. Still have the pineapple with pride of place in the fruit bowl.

June

Do a walk through

Have a walk through your home with a critical eye to make sure anything stands out to you that shouldn't be there. Look up and down because buyers won't want cobwebs, damp patches on the ceiling or carpet stains.

Monday 2 June

I clean the house again so it is sparkling for the viewing later. The lady turns up on time at 1pm. She is quite small but is perfectly made up with designer gear, make up and jewellery. But as the viewing progresses she is delighted that the main bedroom is big because she has a round bed that would fit in perfectly. Ok then.

The lady goes away happy and liking the house saying that she needs to bring her husband to come and look at it.

Now we need to sit back and wait probably at least 2 weeks before the agents call her for feedback.

Thursday 5 June

I ring the agents for feedback from viewing on Monday. They have not called her yet. They say they will try and contact her and call us back when they have. I suppose though if she was interested she would call the agents for another viewing or to offer on the house.

Friday 6 June

We are still waiting for agents to call. They really can't be that crap at chasing up viewings can they?

She must have been lying about liking the house. She would have rung the agents by now to make another viewing with her husband, surely?

Tuesday 10 June

Still waiting for the agents to call.

Decide to call them. They were just about to call the viewer apparently, what a coincidence. Ok then. Do your job.

They will call me back when they get hold of the viewer.

The agents call back. The viewer thinks the road is too busy and the house is not for her. Bitch. Why would she say that she wanted her husband to see it? Surely you know if a road is busy or not when you make an appointment to view?

Saturday 28 June

Wake up and open the curtains to let the sunshine in to cheer us up. Something looks different. Oh that's it. The For Sale board has been stolen. It was probably used last night as a form of transport or plaything by a drunk trying to get home.

Ring the agents up and they say they'll order a new one. We don't bother looking for the old one, it could be anywhere by now. We sit down to have pancakes for breakfast instead.

The agents ring back after lunch. They have someone wanting to view the house. At last. Some sort of activity. It's a shame they won't be able to find the house properly as we don't have the board up anymore. We book them in for tomorrow at 10am.

Spend the afternoon tidying, cleaning and cutting the grass. Fed up of this now and decide to go a drive. Go to McDonalds and get a latte from the drive through. We remember the new house site with the snobby bitch and decide to have a drive by and see how many houses she has sold since we were there last. Maybe the prices have dropped since we last looked. Private house sale prices are dropping.

We park the car and have a quick look around the small site. All of the houses are now built but not many are occupied. Husband gets his latte out of the car and takes it with him into the show house. Well we didn't get offered a coffee last time from the mega show kitchen and he was thirsty.

Same snotty bitch negotiator in show house. We go through the palaver of taking shoes off again. Instead of boots I have open toe sandals on this time. I take my sandals off and put them next to Husband's gardening trainers. We both get a disgusted look at our dusty feet from gardening but we ignore her. She also stares at Husband's coffee cup. We chat and decide to look at detached house next door to the show house. It already has carpet down so we are reminded to take our shoes off. Bitch. She made a real farce of giving us the key and taking it back off us after looking. Husband made a tune up for her.

> They call me Bitch.
> Di do di do
> I'll give you the key.
> Di do di do.
> I'll take the key.
> Di do di do.

He will grow up. Eventually. We had to make a quick getaway because as we tried to lock up the house Husband dropped his empty coffee cup on the hall carpet. It didn't leave a mark but we wondered if snobby bitch had secret cameras placed around the house and was watching everything we did and listening to everything we said.

You never know.

The prices haven't dropped any and are still very expensive. Other new build sites have been knocking their prices down but this particular builder hasn't. Oh well, they must like their own houses so much they don't want to sell them.

Sunday 29 June

The viewing is today at 10am. The house is still clean and presentable so no need to prep it again.

Note to self
- open the windows so it doesn't smell sleepy upstairs

A family turn up on time. Seem ok at first glance; they turn out to be the family from hell. Their 2 children, a boy and a girl decide to race around the house, chase the dog and the cat and throw pebbles into the pond. In the meantime the man of the outfit, who thinks he may be a housing and financial wizard because he has an Estate Agent friend, quizzes me in the kitchen about the asking price. Disabled dog is a nervous wreck already and is trying to climb up my leg to sit in my arms away from the girl chasing her. Husband has a quiet word with them and then they leave moaning and tutting to themselves.

Don't think they will look again. Wonder what their excuse for not buying the house will be? Don't like the angry person who lives in under the stairs? At least I didn't make a huge effort for them with cleaning and tidying today.

How dare they let their children run around a stranger's house like that. They must live in a right pig sty if their kids are like that at home. Twats. I'm surprised the dog didn't bite the children and the cat scratch their eyes out for being horrible to them.

Monday 30 June

We decide to wait a couple of days to give the agents time to chase up the viewers from yesterday. We know what they will say anyway. They will make excuses that the school is too far to walk to blah blah blah. Don't want to know what they say anyway, they were definitely time wasters. If they want to look at my beautifully decorated and accessorised home they can look on-line instead of wasting our time. Or even buy a home magazine like I do.

I decide to go to the summer house at the bottom of the garden with my home magazines and dream of a perfect house. The dog and cat decide to come with me. I end up putting cat out of summer house on to the garden as she keeps biffing the dog in the face when the dog bumps into her. The dog can't settle even for some treats so I take her back to the house.

What a relaxing time this has turned out to be.

July

Set a realistic asking price

If you are serious about moving on and you want to actually move house within a year you must put a sensible asking price to your house. This is very tricky, too low and buyers will think there is something wrong with the house and too high you won't get viewers over the doorstep. Ask your estate agent's advice on this.

Tuesday 1 July

Have uncovered a web of lies at our Estate Agents.

Husband rang them for feedback from the last viewers. The negotiator looking after us is on the other phone and he ends up speaking with the valuer that came out to see us. Apparently it seems no one has been making any notes at all on our viewers, their position and time and date viewed. Nothing in our file at all. Absolutely empty.

The valuer says he will get to the bottom of this. Too right you will. What are we paying you for?

He calls back later and says that the negotiator has handed in her notice and leaves at the end of the week. She has another job with a different Estate Agency.

It turns out that she has done nothing at all. Not just on our file but others as well. We seem to have wasted quite a few weeks.

Think about changing agents and call one of them that valued the house back in January. They will come out Friday next week.

Friday 11 July

Get up early and clean the house ready for the valuer coming later.

Finally have faith in an Estate Agent. He turns up when he said he would, he doesn't mind the dog pawing at his nice suit trousers and the price they charge will stay the same as he quoted in January. What a nice man.

He tells us what to do with regards to the sacking our current agents and gets the paperwork ready for starting advertising our house from 1st August. We fill in the paperwork and he takes some photos for the house brochure.

Husband and I write a letter to the current agents telling them why we are not happy and that we want to cancel the agreement. Rather than posting it we decide to hand deliver it to their offices tomorrow morning.

Husband queries small flies in the kitchen that have appeared overnight. They seem to be around the fruit bowl.

Saturday 12 July

We drive to the agent's office and hand over the letter in person. The valuer is there. We feel sorry for him because it wasn't actually him but his negotiator that let us down. We decide that if they can sell the house before the end of our contract, which is the end of July, he can keep the sale. We reduce the house price by £5k to help him out. We leave them ringing around all the people that have viewed our house already, if they find the information, and the people on their database.

We decide to have a look round the shops before we head back home, Husband agrees silently. We walk past the offices of the new agents we are signing with and decide to do some undercover detective work on the office. We go in and see how we are treated, if we are offered help etc and if they point out houses in our price range.

It turns out that they were good. Glad we have made a right decision at last to go with them.

Go to McDonalds on the way home for a latte and an ice-cream sundae. These are very nice.

Back home and the flies in the kitchen are multiplying. Husband investigates. It turns out they are fruit flies from the bottom of the rotted pineapple. Apparently you can eat them and they have a use by date. They are not just for fancy. Well I never. I usually buy pineapple all chopped up ready to be eaten in a packet. You learn something new every day.

Tuesday 22 July

Husband rang the new agents we will be signing up to and he sorted the new contract out. At least we had the HIPs pack done with the solicitors so we don't have to have another one done or pay the agents any money. Both the new board goes up and contract begins on 1 August.

No sight on the dulling horizon of any viewers. Also, no sight of a property for us to buy. Crap, crap, crap.

Wednesday 30 July

Old agents said they have rung around any prospective buyers etc but still can't find a buyer. Their board outside the house disappears today while out shopping. The magic sign man has been and gone again in stealth.

Husband decides to cut the hedge tonight while the board isn't there so it looks good for when new board goes up on Friday.

The neighbours' curtains are twitching, they will be wondering what we are up to with the sign going. If they want to know they can ask. Although we may not tell them anything.

August

Be nice to estate agents and solicitors

You may get a surprise and find they are humans too and also need kindness and love.

Friday 1 August

The new board appears magically outside today while out at the shops. The sign man is so quick, wonder if he can pull a table cloth out from under crockery without breaking anything? If he can do that, can he pack and unpack a 3 bed semi without damaging anything?

We receive the new house brochures in the post today. They look more professional than the last lot we had. Very pleased with them. And there are no mistakes in them. I sign the form and walk to the post box to post it back to them.

Monday 4 August

Quiet all weekend. No viewers wanting to look around or offer vast amounts of money for our house.

Get a call from an agent selling a property which we have viewed before. Apparently the vender really needs to sell now and is about to go to rented and has people ready to sign up with an agreement. We decide to view again and make appointment for tomorrow evening.

I ring the lovely mortgage people and get different sets of figures from them for a mortgage using different scenarios. They are very patient and must be really fed up of us now.

Tuesday 5 August

Got a viewing today, quite excited.

The house is on the doctors' surgery estate but looks quite pretty and has a double garage for Husband. House is split level over 4 floors. We like it because it is different. The garden is full of bright summer flowers and looks very tidy. There are roses in all of the flower beds. The man selling is very proud of his garden. During the viewing he rushes us around the house, bedroom, bedroom, living room etc and then spent more time in the garden than in side of the house.

The kitchen is a modern one which is surprising because all other kitchens on this estate are slightly newer than a caveman's. Bathroom is not new. The colour scheme is black, grey and white, tiled all over. Oh my god. It is very dark and not very clean. It isn't very big so I suppose it wouldn't cost that much to replace it. The downstairs cloak is also dated having a beautiful turquoise colour toilet and sink with matching walls. It feels like walking into a cold storage room.

Feel slightly bad when the vendor's 16 year old son has to keep leaving a room while we look in it. He has a knack of leaving a room and going straight into the room which we go to next. He seems a bit pissed off with this but then again do they want to sell the house? Shouldn't he be out causing trouble at his age any way?

153

The house has amazing views from the back over countryside and the motorway. It is nearer however to the shops which is a plus point for me.

After chatting with the vendor for a little while we head off for a latte to compare the house with our wish list.

Dream house wish list
- Detached - **yes**
- country/quiet location – **no, suburbia**
- en-suite/cloaks – **yes, cloaks**
- large garden - **yes**
- safe garden for disabled dog and cat – **no, gaps under conifer hedging on back garden and no fence at all at the bottom but can be fixed**
- Parking - **yes**
- larger rooms – **yes, some of them are bigger than what we have now**
- views – **yes, at the back of the house**
- utility (ironing room) - **no**
- not on a busy/main road – **no, back garden is onto a really busy road**
- have some character/old – **yes, suppose 4 storey can provide character, no, built in the 1980s**

The vendor is really desperate to sell. He would rather sell than rent because he is moving to Australia so wouldn't want the hassle of having ties in the UK. We think about offering on it.

Wednesday 6 August

Agent calls for feedback on split level house, tell them we like it but haven't sold ours yet. We will keep in touch. We asked them to let us know when he has an offer on the house.

Think of lots of scenarios in which we could buy the house. We still haven't sold ours yet. We try to work out if we could afford to buy the house while still having ours and come up with a figure which is quite low but what can we do? If he wants to sell, at least we are serious.

I ring the lovely mortgage company to confirm our figures and just check everything would be ok.

It's official. We can buy the house while still having ours. It will be a big mortgage but it can be done. It could work out alright doing it this way. There's no way that I would use that bathroom and it will give us chance to do the new house up while still living in comfort of our house while trying to sell it. It could be an option anyway.

I ring up the agents selling the house and offer on it. I explain to the agents that this is the only offer we can make because we haven't sold ours yet and we will be at our mortgage limit.

Very nerve racking; we might see something else we'd prefer as soon as the offer is accepted. The agents tell me that the vendor would need to speak with his wife who is already in Australia and it would take a couple of days.

Just need to wait now. Am getting quite good at waiting now.

Thursday 7 August

It suddenly hit me today while vacuuming around the cat that happens to be cleaning her unmentionables in the middle of the living room, what an excellent shopping opportunity this new house is going to be if the offer is accepted. Immediately I turn the vacuum off and sit down with notebook.

Note to self
- make a list of rooms in the new house and what needs doing in each
- get wallpaper samples
- get paint sample cards
- collect catalogues from shops
- start making mood boards for the different rooms

Friday 8 August

Oh my god! Sat watching daytime TV when phone rang. It was the estate agents. The vendor has accepted our offer on the split level house. He says he needs our word of honour that we will go ahead with the sale and not leave him in the lurch because he had some tenants lined up ready to sign for renting the house.

Action stations. Call Husband. Call mortgage people. Call bank to make appointment to get some extra mortgage advice, going in to see them next week. Call solicitors. Call the agents back. We want to have another look around the house to remind ourselves. The vendor can't make this weekend because he is having a party...... Make viewing for Monday.

Sit down with a bag of chocolate buttons for a rest. Need to tell neighbours next. Will wait a bit longer until we definitely know something is happening.

Just got to sell our house now.

Monday 11 August

The day seems to take forever to get to 7.30pm when we view our new house.

The vendor is still vacuuming when we get there, we can hear it through open windows. House still good, vendor is pleased he has a sale. He takes us around house really fast again and then into the garden where we linger. He picks a plum from the tree in his garden for us to eat.

Get home with a latte and ice cream sundae and make a list together of things that need doing.

- decorating each room
- new carpets
- new banisters on stairs (to make it more modern)
- new bathroom suite
- new cloaks suite
- new gas fire (other one has been condemned)

At least 3 rooms have laminate flooring so it will be cheaper on the carpet bill.

Tuesday 12 August

Spend the day cleaning our house again to keep it ready for a viewing. Garden still looks ok which is good as it turns out because Husband is really knackered after working most evenings for a month or so.

Go to the bank tonight at 7pm for an appointment with their mortgage adviser. Really nice chap, very funny and very helpful. He has managed to find us a mortgage deal better than the lovely mortgage people who I have kept pestering over the last few months. We sign for the mortgage and leave feeling happy in the fact that one thing is sorted.

We take a latte home with us and decide we need a big push on our house that hasn't yet sold. To do, to do, what can we do?

Wednesday 13 August

I ring up the agents selling our house and ask them if the negotiator dealing with our house can come and look around so she can see what she is selling. She is booked in for Friday to come and have a nosey.

Note to self
- Damn, have to clean house again to make it look really good.

Friday 15 August

Negotiator turns up on time at 10am. She isn't what I pictured from her telephone voice. I imagined her to be about 6ft tall with a scary face and tattoos. It just so happens that she is tiny, and just as lovely in person. On the telephone she is like a Rottweiler who just won't let go of something. She is a great asset to have working for us.

I give her the grand tour of the house making an extra special effort to be nice and she leaves in a positive manner with jobs to do. She said that she would ring around all viewers again to see how they are going and try their database to see if anyone may be interested in buying.

I hope she comes up with something because if we can't sell soon we will have to find someone to rent our house.

Oh my god. We heard that the last people to rent our house before we bought it were a nightmare for the neighbours and wouldn't move out for the landlord. They ended up doing a moonlight flit taking the carpets and curtains with them. Looking at the décor when we moved in, I should think they would have burnt the carpets and curtains, not taken them. They would have been hideous.

One of the stories we heard is that the lady of the house was also a lady of the night, receiving guests very, very late. She also had a minder who slept in his car on the drive at night instead of in the house. And apparently we were an improvement on the tenants because we didn't have loud music blaring out of the bedroom windows in the day time.

I think the neighbours will be very nervous then if we end up renting. Who knows what sort of tenants will turn up. As long as they pay their rent every month and are clean I don't care. Sod the neighbours.

Tuesday 19 August

No news regarding selling our house. Not one single offer. Things are moving with the new house though. Calls and letters forwards and backwards between solicitors and ourselves. Couldn't really work full time and sell a house at the same time, it would be too stressful!

I have let the cleaning go to pot slightly and need to start again. The toilet appears to be turning a yellowy, reddish brown in side, a sure sign that it is ready to be cleaned. I have read somewhere that a can of coke down the toilet before you go to bed helps. May try that tonight.

Note to self
- buy coke from supermarket, none in the house

Thursday 28 August

Got a letter from the solicitors today. They want us to go in to their offices and sign our lives away. Husband in a meeting all day so don't know what days he has free to go and sign with me. Have to wait until he calls me before I can make an appointment with the solicitors.

Decide to look on-line at Laura Ashley, they do sell some excellent stuff in that shop, oh, don't forget Cath Kidston. Spend too long on-line and have spent nearly £250 pound between them on things that would look good in the new house.

Oh dear. Maybe Husband will be out when the deliveries turn up.

Friday 29 August

Ring solicitors today to make appointment for signing. We are going Wednesday next week.

Note to self
- find National Insurance numbers to take with us to solicitors.

Pop to the shops for local housing paper and end up in the bakery buying lunch for one but would feed about 4 people. Just got carried away with the sandwich fillings and cream cakes, they also do gorgeous pasties.

Oh my god. Can't move, too stuffed. Dog is same. She didn't even manage to make it to her basket and fell asleep on the settee at the side of me. There are crumbs everywhere so I will need to vacuum soon.

September

Sell a lifestyle

Remember you are selling a lifestyle as well as
your house. Park a nice car on the driveway, if you
haven't got one, borrow one. Takeaway menus on
notice boards, clean house, wear smart clothes and
say smart things, promote your area, if you can't
do this get your agent to do viewings.

Wednesday 3 September

Go to the solicitors today and sign the paperwork. Our solicitor was quite nice really despite him being a posh dude in a classic stripe tie who you can image plays cricket or horse polo and drinks Pimms every weekend. He says that if we decide to back out of the sale that we have to tell him because the house was bought very cheap and he would buy if from us. We must have made the right decision then.

Note to self
- ring solicitors with National Insurance numbers.

Thursday 4 September

Now we have committed to signing I realise we need some change of address cards, yippee a shopping opportunity!

Go to the local card shop and bulk buy change of address cards and notes. Am so excited! Realise I need some stamps for my recent purchase.

Damn the Post Office. There is a massive queue and the grumpy old twat behind the counter ensures my good mood disappears. Full of old people, the unemployed and push chairs. Manage to make it to the counter to purchase stamps and leave as fast as I can. Hate it in there.

Note to self
- avoid the Post Office at all costs – detrimental to health
- find address book and make a list of people to send change of addresses to
- find a site on-line for notifying utilities etc

Friday 5 September

Right. I prepare the table with pens, stamps, address book and change of address cards. This is my chance to show off with our new house. Look through address book. I can't be bothered to do this now. So boring. It seems like a good idea at the time but I decide to put dog out and wander around back garden with her. Half an hour later, back at the table. Must do this, must write new address out several hundred times. I had read that you can do this online but I prefer to send cards out; they are much prettier than a boring old email.

Three hours later and all finished. Won't stick stamps on yet, just in case. Leave cards piled up on the dresser in the dining room. I just hope nobody sneezes as they will come tumbling down and maybe kill any small animal that happens to walk underneath at the same precise moment they fall.

Tuesday 9 September

Nothing happening at all with our house, it just isn't moving. A few viewers who said they really liked it and want it are still waiting for their own house to sell. First time buyers are struggling getting a mortgage. This is holding up the rest of the chains. I wonder if they have thought about robbing a bank or trying internet banking fraud.

Our lovely sales negotiator is pushing these people but even she isn't getting anywhere. She is staying on top of their every move. It's amazing. She knows when people have their appointments with a mortgage advisor and will then chase the people up who are interested in ours to see if their buyer has had a mortgage agreed. She's great.

We will have to think about renting though. We have decided not to move into the new house straight away. This gives us time to clean, decorate and replace bathroom and cloaks without living in the mess at the same time. Also, our house looks great with the furniture in still for any viewings which may miraculously appear.

Thursday 11 September

Still nothing on the horizon with regards our house being sold. Cheer myself up with a trip to the shops. Decide to pick up lots of wallpaper samples, paint cards and catalogues. Laura Ashley is my first stop. Big mistake. I end up walking out with two big bags of samples, vowing to return when we have the keys to the new house.

Get home and tidy the kitchen cupboards. Start chucking stuff out that has use buy dates from 2006, always knew there was a reason why I struggled making something for tea. Even when the cupboards appeared full, there was nothing in there. Wonder about donating to a Harvest Festival.

Monday 15 September

It's nearly here. We get the keys for our new house this week.

The owner just has to finish packing his stuff up and have one more final leaving party. How many does one man and a teenager need? Bog off to Australia so we can move in!

Friday 19 September

Oh my god! Just left the estate agents after signing for a set of keys for our new house. We now officially own two houses, this is scary. Husband immediately leaves estate agents at speed and we drive to our new house.

We have the alarm code on the back of an envelope with the keys inside and just hope it works.

It does work and we enter our new house. Husband looks at me and decides not to carry me over the threshold of our new house in fear and catching my Ugg boots on the rose bush at the side of the front door. We wander inside and it feels really weird. Doesn't feel like our house; keep expecting vendor to jump out shouting, 'get off my property!' He doesn't though.

After a quick look round the house it is just dawning on us what hard work lies ahead of us, realising that the house needed more work doing than we had originally planned. Owner had left some vases strategically placed with flowers in around the house. How kind of him.

Note to self
- make a list and call 3 different plumbers for quotes
- find a new gas fire to fit hole in surround
- stock up on cleaning materials
- post change of address cards
- find moving guides that have printed off, unless already packed them

We have actually made it! A new house in less than a year, wey hey! Just got to clean, decorate, renovate and move in now.

Oh, we have to find a tenant or seller for our old house now. Not much to do really.

Go back to new house in the evening and start bagging up anything that has been left behind for the tip. There is a strange smell. It must be from the previous owners. Load the boot of the car up with rubbish bags. We will take them to the tip in the morning on our way to the new house.

Go back to house we can't sell and have a bath.

Note to self
- buy air fresheners

Saturday 20 September

Right. Where are my decorating clothes? Find them, peel them apart and get dressed. Husband is already downstairs eating cereals for breakfast. Hope he enjoys them because now we will be on a mission to eat up everything in the cupboards to save moving it. There will be some unusual mixtures for meals to expect, even the dog would probably turn her nose up at them.

Drive to the tip and empty the car boot. There is a funny smell in the car from leaving the rubbish bags in overnight. It is just like the house smell. Drive with all of the windows dropped down. It doesn't work. Arrive at the tip gagging, getting stares from fellow tip rats.

Arrive at new house having had the windows down all the way ready to start cleaning. Husband takes horrible fitted wardrobes out of bedroom one and throws the wood through the window onto the garden. Well, it saves carrying it down stairs to the car. It is already next to the car now I suppose. He makes a start on the bedroom carpet as well, clearing one room at a time. I go through the house taking down all grotty curtains and light shades.

Need a break. Decide to go to fish and chip shop for dinner. Rather than eating it in our new house we take it to our old house to eat where it is cleaner and smells better.

177

We have got a lot of cleaning, painting and changes to make to the new house. Husband calls our electrician to book him in to change a few bits on the new house. Sorted.

We go back to new house and open all of the windows wide to let it air. What is that smell?

We wander around the house trying to find what is wafting around. In the built in fridge I find lots of bits of food and cloves of garlic. The previous owner had not cleaned or defrosted the integral fridge freezer. Maybe this is the culprit. Looking in the fridge it needs burning rather than cleaning. Oh my god. It is disgusting.

More cleaning and stripping crap out of the new house. Had enough now. We lock up and go home. Decide to go to supermarket on way home to pick up some cardboard boxes to make a start on packing non-essential items. You can fit more in a VW Golf than you think. The car is stuffed with boxes. When we get home we store them in the garage. Only now with the boxes and piles of newspapers we have been hoarding we are afraid to go in again. If there is a fire the garage would go up in flames and burn down with 60 seconds I'm sure.

Sunday 21 September

Back at new house cleaning, chucking and stripping out crap. Niece is here today helping us. She means well bless her but she seems to need telling a new job to do every 10 minutes. We send her round the house with the camera to take some 'before' pictures of the rooms and gardens in anticipation of comparing with 'after' pictures. She has taken some good pictures and seems like a pro as we see her in different positions but she also seems to have a knack of taking pictures of you unawares in awkward positions looking stupid. For example, me at the top of the stairs using vacuum cleaner bend over with t-shirt handing low at the front showing off my cleavage. Ta very much.

Note to self
- go through pictures on digital camera and delete unattractive ones of myself

It is now the end of day at new house and we really need a bath to get rid of the house muck, we feel filthy.

Note to self
- remember to put water on timer so there is enough for a bath after a day out. Damn

179

Monday 22 September

Husband booked this week off work so we can get loads of jobs on the house taken care of. We can buy paint etc for when I am painting and he is back at work.

We have booked a person from a DIY store to come out and give us a quote for a new bathroom and cloaks. He turns up and immediately sets his laptop up and plugs into our electricity. I offer him a coffee in a plastic cup and while I make them he is upstairs with Husband measuring the bathroom.

Back down stairs the DIY man gets straight into producing pictures with our measurements while we look through a catalogue and choose bath styles etc. It seems to be taking ages. He came at 10.00am and it is now 11.15am. We told the lady making the appointment that we only wanted a quote and weren't going to sign up on that day. When Husband raised this with the DIY man he seemed to get really narky and packed up his kit after quoting nearly £11,000 for a small bathroom and cloaks for everything including fitting. Husband nearly falls flat on his back after wobbling on his kitchen stool. DIY man can't get out of here quick enough when he knows we won't be signing anything. Sod him, we will find someone else who is cheaper and doesn't look like an eighties throwback.

Pop home for dinner and let the dog out.

When we get back to the new house Husband decides to test the alarm. We have the code and have been using it but still don't know why we have to shut all of the internal doors before the alarm can be set. Husband plays about with it. The alarm sets its self off and the neighbouring curtains begin to twitch in the opposite houses. Damn. The alarm will not work again. Once Husband has put the code in to disable it, a message came up to ring the supplier for a new code. We were going to go to the cinema this afternoon but now we have to try and sort the alarm out.

Husband rings the supplier and apparently we have to pay to get a new code. Sod this. It is a crap alarm system anyway. Husband rings the last company we used and they are coming out tomorrow to install a brand new alarm with new clean sensors, touch pads and an outside alarm box.

Husband calls two more plumbers who will come out to quote on Thursday and Friday.

Eventually get to the cinema much later than anticipated leaving us in the tea time crush of kids after they had finished school. At least it is dark inside and can have a nap if necessary.

181

Tuesday 23 September

Go to buy some paint this morning. Get white for ceilings and all wood work and radiators. Pick up paint cards to help decide what colour to do the walls. Also get some wallpaper samples as I want to wallpaper a feature wall in most rooms.

Back at the new house, Husband is cleaning out the kitchen cupboards and is knackered. They are a mess, all greasy and sticky. He is doing a grand job though. This job makes me feel sick so I am painting bed 4 white all through ready for wallpapering one wall with a black and white city scape wallpaper. This is going to be Husband's office so it needs to be finished first in order to set up phones, printer and laptop to enable him to earn more money for house renovations when we move in.

Alarm men are here and bobbing in and out of rooms leaving ladders all over putting up new sensors. This is so much better. They are in and out quite quick and soon have the new alarm fitted and working. All done.

I pop down to the kitchen to check on Husband just to see if he is flat on his back after banging his head on a cupboard shelf. He is fine, no need to worry but he looks fed up and dirty. We decide to call it a day and go home for a bath. I wrap up my paining roller in cling film and we leave.

Wednesday 24 September

Husband is still cleaning the kitchen cupboards out. I am still painting bed 4 white. I am nearly done now. Last coat of paint on the walls and the ceiling today. I can paint the woodwork tomorrow.

We do our own jobs until lunch time and go home for the nice hot bath we have been looking forwards to.

Go to Homebase to get more paint cards and wallpaper samples. Call in at Laura Ashley as well for wallpaper samples. There is a woman of a certain age in here thinking she is something special and has staff. But really she is giving the sales lady loads of jobs to do getting hundreds of wallpaper samples down and putting them back. We hang around for someone to help while Husband keeps getting the way of the woman who thinks she is special. He is enjoying it and she is not. She keeps giving us dirty looks. Sod you. I bet we will be spending more than you anyway buying wallpaper for about 6 rooms not just for one room, under a dado at that. A lady comes to help and we ask for all the samples we want and don't act like a twat while we ask.

Thursday 25 September

At the new house again bright and early. Bring the disabled dog with us today because plumbers are calling in around lunch time. While she sniffs her way around the new house, casually marking her territory, I paint bed 4 woodwork while Husband finishes cleaning the kitchen. We still haven't found where the smell emanates from.

The plumber turns up and we go through the same as before except he doesn't have a laptop just a notebook and catalogue. He measures up while we look in the catalogue. We choose what we like and he prices up the job. Easy as that. He is more than half the price less than the DIY man and this price includes servicing boiler, taking out old gas fire and a skip on the drive. We tell him we'll get back to him in a couple of days. He seems like a lovely man and his store is local and his price is reasonable.

The disabled dog has had enough of wandering, she can't settle. It is probably that strange smell we can't locate. We pack up and go home.

Friday 26 September

At the new house early and I am painting the woodwork in bed 4. I am going to paper the feature wall tomorrow.

Husband is cleaning all of the laminate floors. We have left the disabled dog at home to get some sleep.

The other plumber comes around lunchtime again to quote for bathroom and cloaks. Again, great like last time. DIY man is really crap in comparison to these two local plumbers. We take his quote home to compare with the first one. The prices are very similar for nearly the same style bathroom.

We go to Laura Ashley and buy some wallpaper. It turns out that a sale has started and we get a good discount off of the papers that we have chosen for the new house. We then go over to B&Q for the city scape wallpaper for bed 4. At least it's not as busy as it is on a weekend here today and we don't have to queue for half an hour. This pleases Husband.

Saturday 27 September

Pick our Niece up at her house nice and early. She is helping me wallpaper today while our Nephew helps Husband bring some garage and shed stuff over in his van. We figure this will make the main removal even cheaper when the time comes because there will be less stuff for them to move.

First things first. My Niece plugs in my iPod and finds the Grease soundtrack for us to wallpaper to. We set up the pasting table and then try and mix the paste up in a pink heart bucket. The heart shape makes it harder to stir because the sides are in and out but never mind. We manage it with only a few lumps left in and begin. The paste table is like an operating table in a hospital theatre with all of the necessary tools all laid out. Roller, blade, brush, cloth, scissors. We happily start wallpapering getting into a good roll with Niece passing tools and holding paper for me. She also turns out to be handy for wiping my hands on her when they are paste covered. She doesn't mind but I know I will have to feed her flying saucer sweets later to make up for it.

Husband and Nephew arrive with the van and start unloading while we put the kettle on. We arrange a picnic of drinks, fruit, chocolate biscuits and crisps to snack on.

They have also fetched over some furniture for the conservatory so we set this up. At least we will have some where to sit and have a drink that isn't in a cloud of dust, muck or smells of paint.

Enough for today and we all head off to the chippy to take back to our house for tea.

Sunday 28 September

Back at the new house and bed 4 looks amazing. It is now finished, painted and wallpapered. It has a laminate floor so everything is ready for moving in furniture now. Cool. One room down loads more to do.

Our Niece is over again helping. In between calls to her boyfriend she is cleaning all of the chrome light switches and plug sockets. I give her all the cloths she needs, show her how to do it and then leave her to it.

Husband and I are taking down all of the chrome curtain rails that were left, cleaning them and putting them back up.

While we are up the ladders we realise that the chrome light fittings that were left are absolutely filthy. We thought that they had frosted plastic around the bulb area but it turns out that this is all dirt. Next job then after the curtain poles is cleaning all of the chrome light fittings.

I call a friend moaning about this extra cleaning and she suggests using baby wipes on them to shut me up. We try this and it works like magic. Turns out you don't need a baby in the house to own some baby wipes. Excellent. It takes some really hard rubbing between Husband and I to get them clean as we have to keep swapping as we keep getting neck ache. I struggle on my turns because I insisted on using the cream household gloves that are like those that doctors wear in

188

hospitals. I wasn't going anywhere near that grime without some protection, other people's dirt makes me feel sick. Don't get me started about all of the previous occupant's hair we keep finding in rooms that have been cleaned several times. Yuck.

Every time I swapped hands with the cloths and baby wipes I get twanged in the face with the fingers of the gloves as they get grabbed with the cloths. Great other peoples dirt in my face. Just what the doctor ordered.

Niece has now finished her cleaning job so we give her a bucket and leather and tell her to clean the windows inside. Bless her. She worked like a trooper in between furtive texts with her boyfriend.

Again, jobs done and we leave for some food.

Husband's week off is over and finished. What a crap week for him, all cleaning and shopping.

Drop lovely Niece off at her house and go home to decide which plumber to use. We decide on the first local one because even though the prices were very similar they could start the soonest. Sorted.

Monday 29 September

Husband calls the plumber first thing and confirms we want them to start. They will start on Wednesday this week. A skip will be appearing on the drive as well this week for the old suite to go in. I can't wait to get rid of that dirt encrusted crap. It makes my skin crawl even going into the bathroom because of other people's hair and soap scum all over. I try to avoid this room.

I am painting bed 1 and 2 today. Doing them white with a wallpaper feature wall in each. The wallpaper I have chosen is a Laura Ashley design to go with other stuff we already have. I turn on my iPod and get going. Husband is working all day so he can't help me.

I paint the ceilings in both then the walls. Had enough and go home.

We come back after tea to look around. It is beginning to feel like ours now with cleaner walls, lights and floors. Leave feeling slightly happier. Depending on how long the bathrooms take we will have to book a moving day.

Tuesday 30 September

Painting again like yesterday, but second coats on bed 1 and 2. I hate painting the ceilings. You can't see where you have been on a second coat because of the white glow and because the ceilings are artexed paint keeps splatting down into my eyes. I may be able to claim disability benefit on account of being blind like the dog.

I have had enough after the ceilings and go home for a bath.

I call a friend moaning about painting and she kindly offers to come and help. What a nice person! She can come over tomorrow for a couple of hours and we will do the second coat of paint on the walls of bed 1 and 2.

Note to self
- book the Oven cleaning man to clean double stainless steel oven (I am not cleaning that myself! Too much dirt and grease, my poor hands are suffering already. They are sticking to everything like Velcro because they are so rough)

October

Write a list and check it twice

Make a check list of features you want in your next house to keep you focused on what is important. Stick to the areas/locations you like and don't be wooed by a house because it has a built in coffee machine you always wanted. Remember most expensive and fancy things will be moving with the sellers to their new house.

Wednesday 1 October

The plumbers are due to start today. We have asked them to do the cloaks first so we can at least have a working, clean toilet while we are doing jobs on the house.

When we arrive at the new house a skip has been placed strategically on the driveway. At least they were clever enough to leave enough space for the garage door to open or maybe that was purely good luck.

The plumbers arrive as I am getting set up for painting and Husband sorts them out while I start. My friend arrives to help but I show her around the new house first. I then make a drink for everyone and then we eventually start painting.

The plumbers have put in the new cloaks suite by the end of the day and they have also been stripping out the old bathroom suite. Excellent. It looks better in there already and the great thing is I haven't had to touch any of it.

Two bedrooms painted, 3 walls in both and my friend leaves to go and pick her daughter up. I give the plumbers a spare key to lock up and change the alarm code to an easy one so they can remember it. I leave ready for another bath.

Thursday 2 October

Because the plumbers are in today doing loads of dusty jobs I leave any painting today at the new house. We leave the plumbers to it.

I decide to start packing up non-essential stuff at home that we can take over to the new house to save money on removal fees. I start on books and stuff in the office. These can then go in to the cupboard in bed 4 which will be the new office because this room is finished. I must remember to use small boxes for heavy big books. I only realise this when after carefully packing up a box being unable to even lift it up. Crap, unpack this and find smaller boxes for this room.

I go into the garage in search of small boxes and end up pulling loads on top of me. I was never any good at Ker plunk as a child. The disabled dog comes in sniffing and stares at me as if to say, 'you do realise that I didn't do this don't you?'

We go over to the new house tonight after tea. We are shocked to find that the bathroom tiles have all been chipped off and have disappeared. The room is completely empty.

Friday 3 October

The plumbers are in again today moving a wall to fit in the new bath. The new suite has been delivered and is spread out in the dining room. We ask if they would keep it in the garage as everyone is stepping over boxes and we don't want any damages or deaths on our hands.

I am painting the woodwork in bed 2 today because the bathroom is opposite bed 1 and there will still be dust around there. Get 2 coats on the woodwork.

The plumbers give us an address for a place they use to buy tiles from and ask us to go and pick some for the bathroom. We will go tomorrow.

Husband calls the electrician who confirms he will be there tomorrow morning. He says he will be there from about 6am. Obviously we don't want to be there at that time and arrange for the electrician to pick the key up from the plumber who actually lives a few doors down from him.

Saturday 4 October

Turn up around 9.30am at the new house and the electrician is just finishing up. He is amazing. We have a new circuit breaker box, any white sockets and switches have been changed to chrome and there is a new outside security lamp up above the front door. He still needs to change the wall lights in the dining room when we find some I like and finish up a few bits so he will return Saturday next week to do this.

We survey our new bathroom. The wall has been moved and there are plastic pipes hanging out of the walls. It looks odd but we presume the plumbers know what they are doing.

We lock up and head over to pick the tiles for the bathroom. Damn. Can't remember if the plumber man said don't get porcelain or ceramic. One is easier to drill than the other. I'm sure the tile men will know the difference.

The tile place is amazing. The trouble is there are so many to choose from. I suppose choosing ceramic or porcelain will narrow it down. We are asked if we want a drink and instantly a proper latte turns up in a cup and saucer.

We can't decide between a grey and cream. Well, I can decide, I want the cream. Husband thinks he wants grey. I remind him that the tiles we have just had chipped off the

198

walls were grey and black at that was the cause of the black hole feeling in there. I smile sweetly at him and he chooses correctly. We order and pay for the large cream tiles and a small brown/cream mosaic border to add a bit of drama.

Back at the new house and Husband is taking up the carpet in bedroom 3 and is lugging it down stairs while I prepare to clean and paint this room.

We are both knackered. Leave the new house with bed 3 ceiling and walls painted white.

Sunday 5 October

Back at the new house. We have Niece with us again.

Note to self
-   buy more flying saucers

The second coat of paint is added to bed 3. Niece is in a foul mood. Husband is washing all of the windows outside and I can hear him keep asking her to do something on average 3 times. She is having boyfriend trouble. We tell her that's the trouble with having a boyfriend with goggle eyes, he always seems like trouble. She is sulking and stomping around. I throw her a chocolate biscuit during our coffee break and this cheers her up slightly.

Back to the painting. I paint the woodwork in bed 3 and bed 1 while the window washers finish up on the back and start on the front. I can still hear Husband cursing under his breath at Niece like he has developed a bad case of Tourettes again. Maybe need to take him to the doctors to have him checked out.

It's a relief to lock the house up and drop Niece off at her house. She has been hard work today and is known to be sweeter.

Monday 6 October

I stay away from the new house in the day and resume packing boxes up. The blind cat and disabled dog are a real help with this. Not. The cat keeps either sitting on the packing paper or hiding in a box. I only find her hiding in boxes when I start putting things in and she jumps out like a Jack in a Box with her tail all bushy. The dog also keeps sitting on the packing paper and licking her unmentionables again for the 20th time today.

Roll on moving day that will be fun.

Note to self
- book the dog into kennels for moving day
- find the cat a box that she can call home

We go over to the new house and run up to the bathroom. The walls are now plastered and are all smooth and beautiful looking. Can't wait for the new suite to be fitted. We have chosen a modern square design with a shower over an L shaped bath.

The tiles have been delivered today and have been neatly stored in the dining room again. We unpack a couple and gaze over their beauty. I was right. Cream was the best colour.

Wednesday 8 October

The plumbers aren't in today but the Oven cleaning man is.

The oven cleaning man works on the oven for about 2 hours scraping and wiping. At the end the oven looks like a brand new one. All this for about £30. It is so much easier to keep clean when you are starting from a clean one. Although it was hard work making conversation with him. In the end I went and sat in the conservatory with a few magazines which I have conveniently brought over.

Husband pops out side and for some reason he wants to go in the garage. Oh my God. We realise that the plumbers have left the garage door unlocked with about £4,000 worth of bathroom stuff in there. Chuff me. Husband's face takes on a very black look and them he disappears to the car to give the plumbers a bollocking. Husband very considerate as oven man is still finishing off in the house and he didn't want to scare him.

We leave when oven man does and go home to pack up some more boxes.

We come back to new house after tea and paint the woodwork in bed 1, 2 and 3. Make a start on painting the doors as well. Husband kindly goes around all of the upstairs doors and removes the handles oiling them where necessary.

Thursday 9 October

I keep out of the plumber's way today as they are installing the suite now the plaster has had time to dry. I pack some more boxes at home. I didn't realise how much crap we still have after sorting through everything about 2 times already. Husband is hankering after a more simple life like living in caravan with no belongings. What he actually means is none of my crap or my hundreds of handbags and several mountains of clothes.

It is late night opening at John Lewis so I persuade Husband to take me to look at wall lights to see if I can find a nicer alternative to the ones that are up. When we get to lighting department we find that some men are changing the display, putting up new stock where the other stuff is sold out or in the sale. Oh my God. Can't believe that one of the designs of the new stock they are fixing up are exactly like the ones I want to get rid of. They happen to cost £20 each as well. There are 3 like this in the dining room and 4 in the lounge. Crap. Husband is pleased as he thinks he doesn't have to spend money. I don't like the other wall lights on display so we leave with me in a very grumpy mood.

I moan and moan in the car so we pop to Asda and find some really nice wall lights for the dining room which are quite cheap as well. They have a crackle glass ball on the end of each arm which will match the flower head on the Laura Ashley wallpaper I have picked.

203

We go to new house after tea to see what the bathroom looks like. We also have to decide what to do with the gas fire in the living room. We can't choose between putting the surround with the fire in the skip or keep the surround and just get a new fire. We have to decide quick if we want to get the fire surround in the skip as it goes in a few days.

The bathroom is looking good. Bath, toilet and sink are in place. Excellent. Oh my God. I go into bed 1 which has been painted all through and ready for papering and see the plumbers have kindly left us several dirty, dusty rubbish bags leaning against the freshly painted walls. Twats. Husband's face takes on that black look again like lightening is about to strike.

Go to B&Q and Homebase to look at and price up fires and surrounds. We did measure the size of hole we have got to fill with the new fire if we keep the old surround but I can't seem to find it in my handbag. Husband's Tourettes begins again but suddenly stops when he realises he has them still in his jeans pocket and didn't even give it to me. Typical.

Oh my God. I think we will be keeping the surround after all. It is cream marble with an orangey coloured wood surround.

The price of the marble is a couple of hundred pounds at least even without a surround. I'm sure I could do something with a tin of varnish and a brush to save some money.

Friday 10 October

The plumbers are in again. Husband calls the office again and speaks to the main man to complain about the sacks of rubbish which were left in bed 1. He apologises and says it will all be gone. I should think so. The skip is on the drive anyway. What lazy sod couldn't be bothered to walk down a few stairs with the sacks and put them in the skip?

Go to the new house after tea again. Husband paints some more doors while I try to improve the fire surround. After I clean it up and paint it with a brown varnish it looks much better. The marble is now shiny clean and the wood surround doesn't look orange anymore. We decide to keep this and just replace the gas fire. Sorted and a much cheaper option, not to mention better for the environment.

Saturday 11 October

The electrician is here again finishing off. He is so fast but his work isn't shoddy which makes a change from usual workmen. He found the wall lights we left for him to put up in the dining room and they are already done. They look really good, well, as good as any wall light can look when I prefer ceiling lights. You can always get fancy ceiling lights, chandelier style with beads and droplets which are much better than wall lights. Also, the problem I find with wall lights is they limit where you can hang pictures.

We are in wallpapering mode today. Husband and I set up paste table and equipment. We paper a feature wall in bed 1 and bed 3 today. I have chosen a pale grey and white paper for bed 1 to match with white furniture and grey silk throw I already have. Bed 3 is going to be my office/room and I have picked a pink flower head on a white background, both on sale from Laura Ashley.

Husband makes a good wallpaper helper. He is quicker at handing me stuff while I am up the ladder with the top part of the paper resting in my head before cutting it. He also helps me down the small step ladders like a gentleman.

It's a good job he is ok at this because we are papering the feature wall in bed 2 tomorrow.

Sunday 12 October

The drill is the same as yesterday. We set up the equipment and paper a feature wall like our lives depended on it. I chose a red and white toile paper for bed 2. I love the French look and already have several throws and bits with the toile pattern on from Laura Ashley.

After a few strips of paper had been put up I was reaching behind me for Husband to put the roller in my hand to flatten the edges of the paper when I realised he wasn't there. I turned around and saw him pondering the wallpaper. He said, 'have we put this paper up wrong?' (It is very kind of him to say we not me).

I stood at the side of him and we both stared at the paper carefully. I said, 'I matched up the sheep's bum exactly on each strip.' After several minutes we realised the paper took 3 strips to return to the repeating pattern instead of the usual two. Husband was totally impressed. Me not so much. I just wanted to finish the papering and go home for a bath. My legs were aching and I felt sticky everywhere due to the fact I had wiped my paste hands on my legs and t-shirt which had then transferred to my arms etc leaving me looking like a giant snail trail.

When we were finished the overall look was excellent. Just what I have wanted, a red and white bedroom. Now I just had to persuade Husband that we need some new white wardrobes I had seen in Argos to finish the look.

Monday 13 October

The plumbers in today doing the tiling in the bathroom. Can't wait to see what it looks like. Not going in today. Husband and I will go to the new house tonight and paint the lounge ceiling. I'm not keen to go in alone with strange plumbing/tiling people in the house. I get on with some more packing with the help of the lovely dog and cat.

Husband eventually gives in and lets me order the white wardrobes from Argos. He agreed when I forcibly told him that our own pine wardrobes would collapse if we moved them one more time and how good the new ones would look as they have a bit of pine to match the pine bed and bedside cupboards. Sorted. I ring up today and order them. A two door and a three door wardrobe. They will fit the gap in bed 2 wonderfully. I will naturally have the three door wardrobe. They will be delivered on Saturday. That's not bad. Husband can have the weekend putting them together, what fun. I already anticipate an outbreak of his Tourettes.

I get a coat of paint on the living room ceiling tonight. The tiling in the bathroom is looking good. It just needs finishing around the sink for the splash back tomorrow.

Tuesday 14 October

Oh my God! We got to the new house just in time. We thought we would go and say hello to the plumbers and check on their progress. Well, check up on them really. We were just entering the bathroom when the plumber was tiling the sink splash back. Blimey. He had put them up the wrong way and it looked really stupid. Husband immediately tells him to take them off before they set and shows him the way we want them. That is the way that we showed him a couple of days before. The plumber then says he needs more trim if we have the tiles that way so Husband sends him off to the hardware shop up the road to get some.

We wait until he does it properly and then feel that we can leave.

We go back to the new house tonight. Had a wander around, everything is looking good. At least the tiles in the bathroom are now they are how we want them. I paint the second coat on the living room ceiling and Husband paints the stairs and landing ceilings. Go home tired again.

Wednesday 15 October

I ring a few removal men to come out and quote. One can make this afternoon. Great, it gets one over and done with. Another quotes general prices over the phone as they just provide vans per hour/day with 2 men. Don't think this will be enough man power for the day. Have they seen how much stuff and crap we have? Obviously not because they don't come out and look.

A man from the removal company comes out this afternoon and as he wanders around he is making lots of notes in a little notebook. He may be staking us out to rob us. He is a likeable man, short, round and grey. Maybe he is a Father Christmas stand in and is making a note of where he can hide presents for people. He says, 'you have a lot of stuff.' I am about to say, 'why thank you kind sir,' when Husband and man start a rant about how much there is and how much it will cost to move it. Oh my god, talk about ganging up on someone. Santa says he will send written confirmation through the post, hopefully today.

We go to new house tonight and check on bathroom. It is looking really good now. The suite is in now with the taps fitted. Because it is new plaster Husband starts painting the ceiling white with bathroom paint and I paint the lounge walls. When we have finished our respective areas we both move on the painting the stairs and landing ceilings. Husband realises he needs to enter a

212

shop soon as we are rapidly running out of white paint and lounge paint. The shops shut at 9pm so we will go tomorrow night and stock up. We go home and have a much earned bath. At least the water is warm this time.

Thursday 16 October

Go over to new house tonight to do some more painting but we call at Homebase first for more paint. We have discovered the points card they have and now they have two more loyal customers. We grab a trolley and go round at break neck speed with strange stares from other customers because we are in our painting clothes. Sod you all. We may look odd but not as odd as you. Who makes an effort at dressing up to go to Homebase? It doesn't make you look rich it makes you look like twats.

Get out of the shop before Husband begins to hyperventilate at being in a shop. Take him back to the new house and instruct him to paint in order to calm down. It seems to work until he realises he has a paint brush in his hand rather than a cup of tea. After a well earned tea break he restarts his jobs.

Husband is painting the bathroom ceiling again and the walls that aren't already tiled. I am painting the lounge walls again, the last coat hopefully. I am going at top speed so I can start the stair walls. I am on the small 3 step ladders so I can edge the wall up to the coving. The next thing I know is my head is hurting and the wall light is on the floor all smashed up. Damn. I have knocked off and broken the beautiful wall light as I lifted up my head from loading my brush up ready to edge the wall. Husband comes running downstairs after hearing the noise and just stands there in amazement. 'How on earth have you managed to break the light?' he asks. So much for his concern, good job I am not dead. He doesn't wait for my response and says, 'it's a good job the electrician saved the lights from the dining room that he swapped for us.' (They were all the same that's way I wanted to change them). Husband disappears to the garage and brings another one in to replace the broken one. He gets his screwdriver and sends me to put the kettle on while he swaps them round. At least I get the pleasure of chucking the broken one in the skip. It makes a lovely smashing sound as it lands on the horrible bath.

The lounge is finished, the bathroom is drying and the stairs are drying so we leave exhausted and feeling a bit sore. I am getting excited now as the day is nearing when I get my lovely new wardrobes.

Friday 17 October

I am waiting around for the next removal man to come and quote. I decide to fill some more banana boxes we have got from the supermarket. The box pile is getting bigger by the day and there's still loads left to do. Although the blind cat is enjoying herself playing one person hide and seek. I'm just glad she is now bored with helping me. Maybe when we pick a removal company they will provide us with bigger boxes.

The removal man turns up on time and is the opposite of the first one. He is tall, thin and pointy. He is still nice and wanders around following me making notes like the first one. This man shows me pictures of covers etc they use to protect mattresses, chairs and settees. He tells me a crew of 2 men will be sufficient. To save me money he thinks that if they fill the van up and then bring it over to new house and unload, doing this until the old house is empty. It will be done in a day with two men apparently. He tells me the quote should be with me by tonight or tomorrow morning.

Back to the new house tonight again. I am painting the woodwork now in the lounge and finishing the walls on the stairs. Husband is still in the bathroom painting ceiling and walls again. The heated towel rail is now up in the bathroom and the old radiator has gone. It is looking wonderful in there now.

The old gas fire has now been taken out of the fire surround and has been chucked in the skip. We now have to locate a new fire that fits exactly in the old hole. This is going to be interesting. Finish painting, down tools and head out to Homebase to look at gas fires. We hit this shop first and then move on to B&Q as that shuts at 9pm. The range in both shops is dismal. There is very little that will fit our gap and we aren't keen on cutting a bigger hole. We pick up brochures and head home. I think the dog and cat will be turning feral soon.

Saturday 18 October

The new wardrobes are coming today. We have an afternoon time slot so we pick up our Niece and head off to a local fire place shop. We are just going to compare prices and styles. The man is late opening the shop so we take an instant dislike to him. He is also not that helpful. He would rather us look around first before we give him our measurements than point out fires that will actually fit our gap. His prices also seem to be really hiked up.

Niece is being positive and drags us upstairs to see what is up there. She is in a good mood today which is surprising as she still has a goggle eyed boyfriend. After wandering around we head back downstairs where the shop man is helping a couple pick a fire. Sod him. We just leave. After all, why should be spend Husband's hard earned money here when he can't be bothered to help us. We have out painting gear on again. Maybe he thinks we can't afford a new fire because we haven't dressed up for the occasion. We make a mental note not to shop here again.

We head over to new house and wait for wardrobes to come. Make a cup of coffee and dig out the chocolate biscuits and flying saucers. I paint the woodwork in the lounge ready for papering the feature wall tomorrow.

My mobile rings and it is the wardrobe men. They are an hour early but ask if we are in to accept delivery. If we weren't ready I wonder what they would have done for an hour to occupy themselves. We tell them that's fine and wait for the doorbell to ring. Two minutes later and here they are. They ask us where we want them and we show them bed 2 which is up a small flight of stairs. Their faces drop and they both say in unison, 'we're not allowed to take deliveries up stairs.' Ooh err mrs.

I reply, 'I asked the operator when I ordered if you would deliver up stairs and they said that yes you would.' After sweet talking them and offering cups of tea they eventually give in and take the flat pack boxes upstairs to bed 2. I mean, it's not as if they were all made up. The wardrobes are all flat packed and with two men easy to carry up 7 steps.

Thank god they have gone. Niece and Husband proceed to unpack the double wardrobe and leave the 3 door wardrobe in bed 4 out of the way. I finish painting the woodwork and then help them.

After lunch at the chip shop we have to take Niece home. We drop her off and head back to the wardrobes. At the end of the day the double wardrobe is up and standing in place with just the doors left to go on. We go home for a break.

After deciding there is nothing on the TV we head back to the new house and put the doors on the wardrobe and clear up the mess. One wardrobe down, a bigger one to go. What fun.

Sunday 19 October

We are wallpapering the feature wall in the lounge today. Any time after this is allocated to putting the 3 door wardrobe together. We set up all of the equipment for papering. We are experienced at this now and it doesn't take long. Looking at the wall together we decide to put the kettle on first while Husband takes off the wall lights so I can paper right up to the holes where the wires come out of.

After a long break we get started. Husband is now great as a wall paper helper and I ask him if he has considered a job change. He ignores me. We both are now getting really fed up of decorating. We realise that the metallic pattern is smudging when we touch it with paste hands and have to be extra careful.

After stopping for dinner and a few more hours later the feature wall is finished and we head home. At least the lounge looks good and the stained fire surround matches.

We will finish the 3 door wardrobe in the evenings now.

Monday 20 October

Up bright and early and at the new house dragging the old washing machine that was left when we bought the house into the skip before they take it away. We find out what one of the smells was that was lingering. It is a big old grey sports sock that has been left in the washer. Oh my god, I'm not touching that. The plumber turns up just at the right time and helps Husband take the washer the rest of the way to the skip from the front door.

In the evening we go to B&Q to get the new fire. After comparing the leaflets, fires and prices the one that fits the hole we are left with the best is in B&Q. We would rather buy from Homebase but this time they don't have what we need. We do buy a fire guard from Homebase though to stop the disabled dog and blind cat walking straight into live flames and setting themselves on fire.

In B&Q we pick the box from the shelf ourselves after looking for a member of staff to help after wandering around for 10 minutes. They all seem to have disappeared when help is needed. We pay for the fire and leave. We take the fire back to the new house and leave it for gas man to fit tomorrow.

Have a look at the integral fridge freezer. The time is drawing nearer when I have to tackle cleaning this monster. I take out all of the shelves and drawers and put them in the dishwasher and we leave. These should be nice and clean by tomorrow when I will start defrosting and cleaning the rest. I am not looking forwards to this job. There were garlic cloves, green herbs and lots of stains in here when I first looked in here. We did check out prices for a new one but it would cost about £1000 for a new one and we couldn't afford this.

Go home and have nightmares about being enclosed in a white smelly box.

Tuesday 21 October

Get to the new house and see that the new fire is fitted and looking good. Try to start it and nothing happens. Try again. Crap. The gas fitter is promptly called and he says that the fire doesn't work. Trust us to pick a box off the shelf of about 6 and get the broken one. The gas fitter says we need to call the manufacturer from the guarantee so they can send someone out to get it fixed.

One hour later and one irate Husband, an engineer is coming out to have a look at the fire tomorrow morning at 8am.

Go home and pack more boxes. We need to come back later and defrost the freezer overnight it is that bad.

Back at the new house and rubber gloves at the ready, I spread out my ingredients of bicarbonate of soda, white vinegar and water. While the freezer is defrosting I begin to wipe out the inside of the fridge. It stinks in here. Keep having to come out for air every 30 seconds. Husband is on mission to find out what still smells from this vicinity. He unscrews the fridge doors from the cupboard doors and we realise what it is. A spill of gigantic proportions has happened and the man who lived here before didn't bother cleaning it up. It was sort of brown and purple and very sticky. It takes about 15 minutes of keep wiping and cleaning my cloth to remove the offending smell and stain. Back to the defrosting.

The boxes and shelves from inside the fridge need another clean despite being in the dishwasher. Do these again in the sink and leave them to dry. Leave the freezer with loads of towels on the floor and a bowl to catch the water and head home. Have had enough now. I will finish cleaning the fridge again tomorrow with the freezer when it is defrosted.

Wednesday 22 October

We are bright and early at the new house to meet the engineer who is here to fix the new gas fire. After in initial inspection it is something to do with the switch to start the flame, it is not making contact or something. Husband knows what the man means but I just nod knowingly. After looking at the fire again the engineer finds that the gas fire has been secured into the surround using silicone sealer instead of the assorted screws included with the fire. Crap. Husband rings gas man to complain. Engineer has finished now and fixed the faulty starter but before he goes he leaves a 'Danger' label on the fire which can only be removed when the gas fitter has done his job properly. He can't come out again to fix the fire until tomorrow. In the meantime Husband calls the gas man's boss to complain as the job he did was not safe.

Back at the new house tonight to finish cleaning the fridge and freezer out. I go through several pots of bicarbonate of soda and white vinegar but eventually feel it is good enough. Well, had enough of doing it. I will keep everything in Tupperware boxes inside the fridge when we move in just in case.

Thursday 23 October

The gas fitter is back out at the new house today, he can't seem to apologise enough. He should have done his job properly in the first place. I wonder what made him rush and glue the gas fire in instead of using screws? Maybe there was some family emergency or probably he was going to the pub for dinner.

The fire is all fixed, screwed in and working again with the Danger sign a distant memory. Thank God for that.

Back at the new house in the evening and we are painting door frames, skirting boards and doors in different areas through the house.

Friday 24 October

Have a day off painting, will go in tonight. Do some more packing at home. We have decided on the removal men we want and I give them a ring to confirm and pay them over the phone by credit card. We have picked a moving day. It will be Tuesday 11 November. This will hopefully encourage the plumbers to finish off and clear off and give us a goal to work towards with decorating. Also, it will be cheaper to move on a Tuesday.

At the new house, I am painting wood work again and Husband is measuring rooms for carpets. We only need carpets in the lounge, stairs, hallway and bed 1 and 3. We have decided on lino for the bathroom and cloaks as it will be cheaper than tiling and easier to take up if there is a problem like a water leak etc.

Husband has finished measuring the floors and gives me a scrappy bit of paper with all of the measurements on for safe keeping. I know if he keeps the measurements we will never find them again. I quickly put them in my handbag.

Saturday 25 October

Off for 9am to the local retail park to check out the carpet shops. Oh my God. It is a god awful place to be, and not just because it is the weekend. The first shop we go in we begin browsing the carpets on long rolls, not dissimilar to giant sausage rolls when an old man shuffles up to us and asks if we need any help. We give him the measurements and tell him we want a plain carpet and one that is easy to clean as we have pets. He shows us a few carpets which we like and then he asks us to sit at his desk while he works out how much we will need.

Husband and I are sat there really quiet staring around for what seems like ages watching families browse and kids run and fall with carpet burns as a result of their misbehaving. The man is taking ages trying to work things out without a calculator; it seems he is now a relic and maybe should be extinct like the dinosaurs which he is similar in age to.

At last he has finished and gives us a price. We were thinking about £1000 for 3 rooms and the stairs. His quote is double. Husband and I stare at each other with our mouths open. It's not like we have picked expensive carpet either, it's only £5.99 a sq. metre. Blimey. The old man is staring at us. I think he is expecting us to be grateful that he has worked it out for us without a calculator. Ta very much. Husband says, 'it is a little more than we were planning to spend and

229

you're the first shop we have been to.' Old man continues staring. Husband continues talking, 'we need to check out other shops but thanks for giving us a price.' With this, the old man throws the bit of paper we have with our measurements on back at us, actually to our faces and storms off. Well tries to storm off as well as he can with a shuffle. Sod you then, I thought the customer was always right.

Oh my God. What a twat. We will not be going there again for anything. We really dislike this big named carpet shop and try to think of smaller companies around us.

Enough carpet shopping for now, it is dinner time and I feel well ready. We go to the chip shop. We should get a discount the amount of times we have used the chippy while renovating the new house. Maybe even an extra scoop of chips.

Note to self
- big smile when ordering fish and chips and ask the server how she is

We remember a small carpet shop that we have seen in a nearby village and head over there to look at what they have. Get there about 1.10pm and find they close at 1.00pm. Never mind, we will pop in during the week.

We go back to the new house to paint more woodwork. Yippee.

Sunday 26 October

Had nightmares last night of grey haired old men floating around on carpet rolls throwing stuff at me. So glad we didn't give him our business, old sod, is he that old that he has forgotten all of his manners?

We have had enough of houses, painting and papering. We go to the cinema this morning to forget everything and to be entertained. Excellent.

Go to another big carpet shop this afternoon just to compare prices with other old man shop. It was a younger man in his 40s and he was much more polite and they were offering discounts. We have found a good carpet that can be cleaned with bleach etc and not stain anywhere from the cleaning products you use. This is very good news with a dirty cat and dog. He gives us a price after quickly working out how much we will need. He has come in at £1500 which is much better but we still want to check out the small local carpet shop to see what they can offer. We thank him for his time and go to the new house to paint doors and skirting boards. At least having plastic windows saves me from painting the frames. Oh my god! Look at the state of the frames, they are filthy. Send Husband round with his car washing bucket and leather to wipe all of the frames down.

Monday 27 October

The plumbers are finishing today hooray! They realised we were serious about our moving in deadline and knuckled down to it. The only thing left to do is fit the bath panel when the lino is down. One of the plumbers decides to cut the bath panel to size ready to go straight in when the lino is down. Oh my God! After lots of measuring and up and down the stairs he cuts it too short. He immediately gets on to the boss man and another panel is ordered. We also tell him that we don't want silver heads on the screws that show on the front of the bath panel, they look odd. We want white so they don't stand out and so they match the bath panel. The plumber decides to go and buy these from a local shop and promptly disappears for about 2 hours.

Painting the bathroom walls and ceiling with special bathroom paint, damn it's hard work painting on new plaster. I manage to get two coats on the cloaks ceiling today as well, it may seem like I've worked hard but it is only very small.

Our plumber returns with white ended screws, leaves them and goes home. Job done. We are to give them a call when the lino is fitted and they will fit the new bath panel.

Tuesday 28 October

We arrive at the new house and the skip is finally gone. Well, apart from the sticky looking dribbles it has left along the driveway. What has been put in here that has leaked? We now await lots of rain to rinse this off the drive.

Painting doors again. How many doors are actually in a house with some open plan rooms? The doors have all needed 3 coats of paint each.

Husband goes round the finished doors and oils and replaces the chrome handles and catches. Things are starting to look good now. We need to paint and paper the dining room, paint the kitchen, finish the cloaks and start the hallway and then we need the carpets down. Not much more to do, hopefully this can be achieved before we move in. We also need to be putting curtain poles up in the rooms which have not had any left when the man moved out.

Pack some more boxes. I am now onto the good big boxes that the removal company has dropped off. They are better than banana boxes from the supermarket. We can stop buying newspapers now for wrapping things in because the removal company also dropped off some paper as well as the boxes.

All this time renovating the new house and we have had no interest in the house we are currently in. All odds are pointing to renting this one out if we can't sell. Husband and I decide to ring a few rental agents for advice and arrange for visits to the house so we can get a rental price and some advice. I ring our house insurers to find out about insurance for the house while we rent it out. They are very helpful and say they will post the quote out to me.

Wednesday 29 October

Start painting the dining room ceiling and coving today. Need to put carrier bags over the new wall lights we had fitted so they don't get covered in paint splats. Husband would not be too pleased if this happened after all of the moaning I did about changing them.

I am nearing the bottom of the paint tin while I am finishing the coving off and I realise that we have no spare white matt paint in the house. There is just enough left in the tin after scraping out the sides to finish the first coat. Cover my paint brush in cling film and now wait for my lift home. Husband dropped my off this morning and then drove away at full pelt. He rings to say he is just getting off the motorway and will be here in about 5 minutes. I wander around the house admiring all of the work we have done shutting all the windows as I go.

In the meantime our Nephew turns up to see if we need any help. I don't know how he does it, he always turns up when we are leaving or have run out of paint. Husband arrives and then we all head off to the chip shop to take back to the unsold house.

In the chip shop car park Nephew is assaulted by an old woman with a walking stick because she reckons that he has parked too close to her car. There is actually loads of room, you could park a motorbike in the gap but she still complains. Husband and I are

235

already in the chippy laughing at him while the old woman waves her walking stick at him.

We go to Homebase and buy yet more paint and drop it off at the new house on the way home. This trip goes ahead without any snags or old people hindering us.

Thursday 30 October

I am at the new house this morning, painting again. The ceiling and coving has its second coat in the dining room and I manage to get a coat of paint on the walls. Again, Husband has done a drop and run on me and I am here painting alone. I turn up the iPod and get on with it. I paint the cloaks walls for the first time after cleaning them of course.

Can't wait for it to be finished now and to move in. It won't be long now. Husband turns up when he said he would and I am ready and waiting on the doorstep with the house all locked up and paint all over me again eager for a quick extraction.

Return this evening with Husband and put up two curtain poles in bed 1. This task goes quite well after we managed to find the tiny drill bit which had lodged itself between bigger pieces and bits of wood in the tool box. I don't know why Husband has kept crappy bits of wood and decided to keep them in here. After Husband has finished I praise him greatly and then mention the shops are still open because we need a roller blind for bed 1 as well as the curtains for the front window. I insist we look after telling him, 'I am not in an American movie and need a black out blind so I don't show the rest of the estate my naked body every time I get undressed.'

He sees my point of view and we go blind shopping. We check Dunelm out and find a lovely silver/grey black out blind for the front window that doesn't need cutting down to size. Husband does a small triumphant dance in the store and we walk to the till. On the way I spot some silver/grey silk mix curtains for bed 1 that will match the blind and have to stop and check them out. It's amazing, Husband offers to buy them as well as the blind, and before he realises what has happened I have picked the correct sizes and we are standing at the till waiting to pay. These curtains will match the grey silk throw I have from Laura Ashley already for this room.

We drop the booty off at the new house on the way past and go home.

Friday 31 October

The dining room needs one more coat of paint on the walls today which I complete on my own again with my iPod blaring out to drown out the boredom. Husband is getting quite good now and dropping off and disappearing but he is also good at extracting me as well at the end of a session. Bless him. I finish the dining room and paint the cloaks walls for the last time.

Had enough and don't go back to new house tonight, we watch crap on the TV instead with cat and dog because it is Halloween. The cat gets scared of loud noises and we figure there will be fireworks going off as well for Bonfire Night because it is the start of the weekend. I have bought several bags of mini chocolate bars for Trick or Treaters but Husband and I end up finishing them off to ourselves. If we get any small people knocking at the door we will just have to give them an apple or something. Our needs are greater than theirs.

November

Remember to buy the worst house on the best street not the best house on the worst street as you can change a house but not its location.

Saturday 1 November

We manage to get to the small carpet shop at last. They are very nice and helpful in here. They also stock the carpet we like that you can clean with anything. They price up a rough estimate but say they would need to come out to the house to measure up themselves. How professional, the larger stores didn't say this. The estimate comes in at just under £1000 which we had in our minds, so far so good. We leave armed with lino samples and different colours for the carpet we have chosen. We wanted to have the same type of carpet throughout the house but with a lighter shade in the two bedrooms. We figure a slighter darker shade would hide any marks on the stairs and in the lounge.

We take the samples back to the new house and place them strategically around. Straight away we pick a cocoa colour for the lounge and stairs and a cream for the two bedrooms. Sorted. The carpet man is coming out to measure on Monday morning so he said he would take the samples back with him then. We just need to decide on a lino for the bathroom and cloaks now. This is harder than you would think. The smallest rooms in the house are taking the longest to decide.

We had originally thought a slate or wood style lino for these rooms but laying the samples down has changed our minds. They both look wrong and hideous at the same time. We think we want a speckled cream lino with tiny bits of silver that sparkle in the

243

light. We have seen something similar in a hotel once. The colours should all match in the bathroom because we have painted a light brown feature wall to go with the cream and brown tiles.

Sunday 2 November

We clean all the laminate flooring again this morning with a special wood floor cleaner and they look so much cleaner. Just need to get up a few paint splats where they have soaked through the dust sheets when I was painting. Husband doesn't agree with me when I call them small splats he thinks they are more like puddles.

We keep popping our heads into the bathroom to look at the lino sample against the painted wall. It still looks good and we think we will go with this.

I start painting the radiators, these will only need two coats so won't take as long as the doors. I manage to paint all of the upstairs radiators today after cleaning them all first. Who knew they needed cleaning first after an initial inspection? Husband just shakes his head at me. He is heading out into the garden to cut the grass before we lose the dog in it. He thinks it will be the last cut before the end of the year.

Monday 3 November

While waiting for the carpet man to come and measure the rooms I am cleaning the windows in the conservatory again. They seem to have sticky bits all over them which have proven too hard to remove the first time. I also clean the French doors into the conservatory from the lounge. I can't believe how much my arms ache. The plumber is upstairs doing some finishing off bits in the bathroom and comes down to tell me he has heard the doorbell go. It is the carpet man. Good job the plumber was here because I didn't hear the bell at all. I feel relieved to have a break. I thank the plumber and usher the carpet man in and put the kettle on. It is time for a chocolate biscuit.

Carpet man does his measuring quite speedily. He is in a hurry so declines the offer of a drink and takes the samples with him and leaves. I on the other hand have a second drink and many more biscuits. I think I deserve the rest. I need to build the strength back in my arms to finish cleaning the windows.

After a long morning, I am extracted right on time again and Husband and I head home.

Note to self
- check the change of address cards, where are they? When do I need to post them?

Tuesday 4 November

Our moving day is nearing so I stay at home and pack some more crap, or should I say our lovely belongings. I really should go and tell the neighbours about our moving day but can't be bothered. I look out for lovely neighbour though through the kitchen window every time I wash up.

I ring the carpet man and order the carpets. We have still not decided which lino to have for the bathroom but this can be done in a couple of days the kind man says. The carpets will be delivered on Thursday to the shop and they will come and fit them on Friday.

We are cutting it a bit close before moving in but it would be preferable to buy new carpets and have them fitted before moving in all of our furniture.

Go to the new house tonight and paint the downstairs radiators, after I have cleaned them of course.

Wednesday 5 November

Back to painting the radiators this morning. I finish the last coat on the upstairs ones this morning and wait for extraction. I find myself in the conservatory browsing through the goods we have purchased but waiting to be dispatched and arranged in their appropriate room when they are all decorated and carpeted. I have the grey silk curtains for bed 1, gold silk curtains for the dining room which we got for £12 from Rosebys because they were shutting down. I have cream velvet cushions with black piping from Homebase for the lounge from a recent sale and gold organza cushions for the lounge and a grey one for bed 1 from B&Q. I can't wait to put things together when the carpets are down. I am looking forwards to putting the new curtains up, never had silk ones before.

We are not going to the house tonight, we are staying at home with the cat to keep her company while the fireworks are going off and plus we are really knackered.

Thursday 6 November

Finish the radiators off downstairs today ready for the carpets being fitted tomorrow. Just in time really, there should be enough time for the paint to harden shouldn't there?

Ring the carpet shop and confirm they are coming tomorrow. Husband has taken the day off as holiday so he can be around the house with me while the carpet men are there. He is so kind.

Friday 7 November

Got a long day ahead of us today with the carpet fitters coming. We get to the new house just before them at 8.15am. Action stations. Their van is unloaded and carpets and grippers are taken to the appropriate rooms. I can't stand the mess already and retreat to the kitchen and put the kettle on. The two carpet fitters start upstairs in the two bedrooms and will then do the lounge carpet and the stairs and the landing at the end with the cut offs from the lounge.

We definitely picked the best colours, cream and cocoa. Husband and I don't have anything much to do so we are sort of wandering around every so often and then going back to the kitchen. Husband then wanders off on his own to chat to the fitters and he ends up helping them by putting bits into black bin liners. I decide to read some magazines. I realise that bed 1 has been finished with the carpet fitters moving onto bed 3. I set up my iron and ironing board in bed 1 and tackle pressing the silk curtains freshly out of their plastic packaging. I might as well hang the curtains up now this room has been finished.

Husband appears with the two light shades for this room from the conservatory and hangs them up for me. We waited for the carpet fitters to finish before we hung them up so they didn't knock the glass beads off the frames.

The curtains are ironed and the hooks have been put on the heading tape. Damn. I can't reach the curtain pole to hang them even on tip toe. I call for Husband and eventually he returns to hang the curtains for me. This room looks fabulous. The first room complete. The silk curtains match the grey and white wallpaper and the whole look is quite French which pleases me. I can tell Husband is also impressed.

It is now lunch time and the carpet fitters have their food in their van on the driveway. Husband stays in the house while I escape and go home to check on the dog and let her out. I bring back an array of foods to form a picnic anyone could be proud of. Sandwiches, sausage rolls, pot of cut carrots, crisps, cans of pop and donuts all courtesy of the local Sainsbury's. When I get back Husband is chuntering again. The carpet fitters have managed to spill a box of tacks on the driveway. They think they have picked them all up. We'll have to wait and see who is the first to get a puncture on the car.

Lunch is finally over with and the carpet fitting begins again. Husband and I iron and hang the curtains in bed 3 when the carpet is down and in bed 2 while we are waiting for the lounge carpet. Things are slowing up now and the two fitters are taking their time on the stairs and landing carpet. At least the lounge is finished now after the long consultation between Husband and the fitters about where the surround sound speaker wires need to be under the carpet.

The house is beginning to take on a new smell of its own, a hint of sweat and new product smell. I open a few more windows.

Eventually the fitters have finished but it is about 6.00pm and both Husband and I are helping tidy up now to get rid of them quicker so we can go home. Knackered again as usual. We have filled about 5 bin liners with rubbish and we are surprised when the fitters actually take them away with them instead of leaving us with their rubbish. Amazing.

Saturday 8 November

We have decided to take my car over to the new house today and park it in the garage. I won't need it now until after we have moved in. I decide to load the car boot up with Christmas presents I have already bought and my birthday presents which I have also purchased for myself. It is my birthday in a few weeks and if I don't buy them Husband will forget.

Husband follows me down to the new house in his car. We stop at the local Sainsburys on the way past and purchase more picnic foods to eat at the new house.

After my car is parked safely in the garage and the car battery disconnected, well, I don't want anyone driving off in it, we head back in side and look at the new carpets.

We decide to have our picnic lunch in the lounge in front of the new gas fire because the weather is now getting chilly. It feels really nice and I can't wait to move in.

Sunday 9 November

Moving day is getting closer and closer now. We arrive early at the new house and set up to wallpaper the feature wall in the dining room. This is a slow job because of the two wall lights that have to be taken down carefully so as to remember how they go back up. I manage to paper around them really good and Husband is really efficient at putting them back up again. Our electrician would be proud of the job that Husband has done.

During our break though Husband isn't as impressed with my handiwork when I throw him a Penguin bar and it hits him square in the middle of his forehead. Crap. A winning smile from me helps Husband recover more quickly as does another cup of tea. I am known for my crap throwing skills. I nearly turned Nephew into a vegetable when he was about 4 years old when a ball I threw to him missing his head by about 2mm and hitting the radiator he was standing in front of. This shook the whole house. At least he can't remember this incident.

The wallpapering is finished by lunchtime and we pack up. The pasting equipment is all dumped in the garage now because all of the wallpapering is now complete. We have decided to paint the kitchen and hallway after we have moved in now rather than rushing. These are easy rooms because there won't be any furniture to move around.

We head off home and pack some more stuff up together.

While packing we saw the neighbours at both sides coming and going so we went out and told them our good news. Well, we were pleased with our news. The neighbour on the adjoining wall didn't look too pleased when we said we would probably end up renting the house out. We don't care though because we won't be able to hear her having sex anymore. What a result!

Monday 10 November

We are moving house tomorrow. Husband has booked this week off work as a holiday so we can get things sorted quicker than if he was working.

I defrosted the fridge and freezer yesterday and this morning we took most of the stuff to the new house ready for tomorrow. We have also got to take the dog to the kennels today ready for tomorrow so she won't get hurt and trip anyone up. Oh my God. She has started her season today. Our lovely neighbour said she looked like she was ready a few days ago. How does she know these things? Should she be looking down there anyway it's very private for a small dog.

The dog is now booked in at the kennels and we get on with taking any pictures down from the walls and filling in holes. We struggle with the huge mirror over the fire place. Well, I struggle because Husband and Nephew put it up. I can feel my arms shaking while Husband is the removing screws. Hope it doesn't fall on him because I need his help tomorrow.

We have a break from packing and drop the dog off at the kennels. We then go and look at the new house. We wander around amazed. We can't believe how much we have done to it since we got the keys in September.

Everything is as packed as it is ever going to be by early evening. We sit down and watch TV with the cat who is feeling lonely without the little dog for company.

Tuesday 11 November

We are moving today!

A massive lorry turns up at 8.30am with a crew of 4 men. What a result. We had booked a smaller lorry with 2 men. They must be short on work today. Husband is really impressed with the lorry because it has a side door and a back door. Everything is just about packed up. We have already been over to the new house and taken the bedding in bin bags so it doesn't get lost and we have something to sleep under tonight. We have also bought some sandwiches etc from our trusty Sainsbury's and put them in the new house fridge ready for lunch later. I am so organised I scare myself sometimes.

The cat is also ready; she has taken up residence for the day in the plastic pet carrier and is being housed in the kitchen out of the way until we are ready to move her to the new house when this house is packed up. She doesn't look impressed with us.

The removal men are really fast and efficient at emptying the house. They bring in wardrobe boxes for emptying the wardrobes into and we realise we need an extra one because the coat cupboard still needs packing up. Oops.

As the men empty a room Husband and I go in to vacuum and dust it. At least they put down carpet protectors before they started but we still find a few dirty footprints on the cream carpets.

We always seem to move in bad weather. It is November, dull and drizzling outside. When we moved into this house 12 years ago it was February, dull and drizzling. Super. We must have a summer move next time.

After many cups of tea and several packets of biscuits the house is now empty. We make sure the removers know where they are going to the new house. We remember to get the cat from the kitchen and lock up. I already have the change of address cards in my handbag and we post them on the way to the new house. We pass the lorry which is parked up in a lay by near a sandwich shop with all of our worldly goods inside and wonder if we should have taken out insurance after all.

We put the cat in the new kitchen and have our quick pre-bought lunch in here with her and await the big lorry. They soon turn up and bring their carpet protectors with them. There is a big decision now because their boots are really dirty and we have new carpets down. They decide that two men will empty the van and two men will stay in the house and take the furniture and boxes to the right rooms. Sorted.

Apart from when it comes to bringing the settees in they won't fit through the front door. Apparently the porch ceiling is lower than the rest of the rooms and the settees won't fit through. Crap. The men begin scratching their heads and trying to figure something out. They realise that if they carry the two settees down the side of the house and lift them over the arched side gate, they will be able to carry them through the conservatory and then into the lounge. Sorted. These men are truly worth their money.

The rooms seem to be stacking up with boxes and furniture. The men have to stop bringing boxes in while they build the beds back up otherwise they won't fit anything more in the rooms.

Several drinks are made while the beds are assembled. We can't actually fit in bed 3 now because the furniture is in but boxes are piled under and on top of the furniture. What a wonderful week off Husband will have helping me sort through all of this.

The younger of the removal men stops suddenly when carrying a box through the dining room and says, 'oh no, I forgot about the 2 minutes silence this morning, it's Remembrance Day.'

It was quite nice that some people still don't forget this, whatever age they are. At least we will remember what day we moved in.

The removal men have had enough now and have been leaving boxes in the dining room instead of taking them upstairs, before quietly slopping off to the van. They have nominated one person to come and check everything is ok before they go. We think about complaining but they have worked hard for their small fee and decide to leave it. Besides, we have also had enough of having them around and are glad to be seeing them leave.

Well, that's it. We are officially moved in now and have lots of fun ahead of us in the next few days trying to find stuff we need. We leave everything as it is and go and pick the dog up from the kennels. When we get back with the dog we let the cat out of her little plastic house and let the two of them sniff their way around the new kitchen.

Because our old house hasn't sold we now need to find an agent and tenants. That can wait for now though. Husband needs to connect the TV and Sky and I need to have chocolate and to put the kettle on.

Wednesday 12 November

Today is spent rummaging through boxes and trying to put clothes away in the new wardrobes which are in bed 2. The boxes that I need first are actually at the back of the room under about 2 layers of other boxes which are all stacked on the spare bed. I eventually get to them and keep chucking empty boxes downstairs for Husband to flatten and put in the garage ready for the removal company to come back and collect them.

After a day of this we decide that because Husband is on a so called holiday that tomorrow we will go out for the day because I can finish unpacking when Husband is back at work next week.

Friday 14 November

It was great to have a day away from the house yesterday, went to the Peak District for a walk and found some ducks to feed with crumbs of cheese and onion pasty and the bread from a cheeseburger.

We have finished painting the bathroom now and had the lino delivered that we chose. It has been wedged into the bathroom to keep it pliable while the fitters fit it. If we put it in the garage it would be too cold and not very easy to fit. So now we are struggling to get around the huge roll and nearly have to do the splits to get out of the bath. Husband rings the carpet shop and they will come out and fit the lino on Monday. Next job after the lino has been fitted is to get the bath panel fitted which is actually in the garage. This is the new panel because the old one was taken away when it was cut too short.

Ring a couple of letting agents about our old house and get some prices. We decide on a local agent from the next village and they will come out to meet us at our old property Friday next week.

Monday 17 November

Start unpacking early while Husband is in his newly decorated office trying to untangle his wires and cables in order to set up his phone, laptop and printer. I have left him to it because if I try to help I get grunted at. An hour later and Husband finds me under a pile of empty boxes trying to flatten them. I have got brown tape stuck all over me and have millions of card board cuts on my hands. It's break time.

The carpet fitter turns up while we are having a break and we send him upstairs to the bathroom. He says it won't take long and appears 45 minutes later saying it is all done. Excellent. We go up to have a look and it looks great, we picked the right colour. Slate or wood effect wouldn't have looked right.

Husband rings the plumbers and they will be round tomorrow to fit the new panel, hopefully cutting it to the correct size this time.

Tuesday 18 November

The plumber is here bright and early about 10am to fit the bath panel. It is a different man than last time who cut it too short, maybe they don't want to buy a third panel. We leave the plumber to it and keep hearing banging and him going up and down the stairs to cut bits off the panel. I so hope that it fits. I also hope they use the white screw head covers on the panel instead of the chrome.

Eventually the panel is fitted and the mess upstairs is cleaned up. At last, everything is finished and we no longer need any more work men in the house. Thank God.

Get back to unpacking boxes, need to finish this because I can't find my shampoo and am using Husband's.

Friday 21 November

Meet the letting agents at the old empty, cold house at 8.30am. She wanders around making notes on the condition of the house and any carpet stains and marks which the tenants can't be blamed for. Husband walks around taking photos of the empty rooms so we can remember how they look when the tenants move out and can prove the condition of them if the tenants need to put something right.

We sign the contract and she leaves saying they will get the brochure ready today.

Husband rings the plumbers up that we have just used on the new house because we need to have a certificate for the gas hob and the central heating serviced. They can come out on Monday next week.

Monday 24 November

The plumbers are meeting us at the old house at 8am to get the house ready for renting out. Because the house is empty we leave them to it after letting them in and call back later.

Oh my God. When we go back to check on the plumbers he says there is a gas leak when he tried to test the system or something. He can't do anything to it because it is on the pipe that belongs to the gas provider and leaves. Crap, things are never straight forward. I think we need another gas fitter, this one is useless. Husband calls the telephone number for gas leaks and they send out a gas man to check on the leak and he can be there in half an hour. At least we don't have to wait very long. Gas man comes and checks the pipes. He thinks that there wasn't a leak and the pipe has been damaged. Great. He repairs the leaking pipe anyway and leaves. At least we didn't have to pay for it but Husband says the plumber will pay. I think I know what he means.

Husband rings the plumber back and tells him it is fixed but now he can't come back out until tomorrow now to issue our certificate. Twats.

The rental house brochure is ready today. They have used the pictures from the for sale brochure so it looks better with furniture in and is set out nicely instead of being empty.

267

I pop to Asda and get some cheap lamp shades for the empty ceiling lights and get curtain poles for the living room and bed 1. We have left all the other curtain poles and blinds up any way. Need to find the old curtains which we gave to Husband's mum and get them back for the living room and bed 1, it will save buying some more.

We go back to the old house tonight and fix the curtain poles up and put up the lamp shades. The house is looking very bare and old without our lovely furniture in it.

Tuesday 25 November

Meet the plumber back at the old house for him to finish off his job that he should have done yesterday without messing up. He can't look us in the eye because he knows he lied about the gas leak and that it was him that caused it. Twat. Anyway we get the certificate and he disappears.

We drop the certificate off at the agents so they have a copy along with a spare set of keys for the new tenants who ever they may be.

We get a call from the agents later in the day that have a couple that want to view the rental house. They want to come tomorrow so we make a lunch time appointment. We will meet them over there because we want to see who they are instead of letting the agents show them around.

Wednesday 26 November

Oh my god. How on earth can this couple afford £600 a month rental on this house at their age? They look about 17 years old with 3 children. We let them look round the house on their own. We wait in the living room sat on the window sill. There is nothing to steal anyway that's why they are looking on their own.

They appear down stairs and say they are finished and leave. We lock up and leave just after them.

Get a call from the agents this afternoon someone else wants to look around the house on Saturday, a woman on her own. We make an appointment. The agents seem to be pulling in viewers, we are impressed.

Saturday 29 November

Arrive at old house and put the heating on. We they go to next door for a chat while we wait. We head back into the house and wait on the window sill again in the living room getting a warm from the radiator under the window. We have now been waiting 20 minutes and the woman hasn't turned up. Bitch. Husband calls the agents to see if she has rung them. She is a no show and the agents haven't heard from her. We turn the heating off and lock up. We call the chip shop on the way home for dinner.

December

Remember when you have sold your house and are ready to move into your lovely new home take your time packing and label everything so you know exactly where it goes in your new home. Good luck ☺

Monday 1 December

       The agents ring again with another viewer. The appointment is made for tomorrow. The agents have tried phoning the no show viewer from Saturday but they can't get hold of her.

Tuesday 2 December

We meet the lady viewer at the house to show her around. She has turned up with her mum who seems to have no sense of humour. They wander around the house on their own, because it is empty and there is nothing to steal. We wait in the living room again.

They find us and ask us a few questions about council tax etc. She says she likes the house but she has a dog. Are we willing to let her rent with a dog? She tells us it is a Labrador. We think that we had a dog here and it should be ok but we will talk to the agents.

We ring the agents when they have left because we are concerned about the damage a big dog might do. We decide to let her dog live there if she wants it. We can always use the bond she will pay to restore any damage done.

We get a call from the agents that she wants the house and can she move in on 19 December. Wow. We agree the moving date and the agents make an appointment for her to go in to sign the paperwork. If we have a tenant in the house over winter we won't have to pay any heating bills to keep the pipes from freezing over, what a result. The agents also tell us that she would like the house for about 2 years.

Monday 15 December

Go over to the old house to check everything is clean and hovered ready for the tenants moving in on Friday.

The house seems so old and I had never realised how bad the cream carpets were when we lived here but now it is empty they look like they need replacing even after we had them cleaned. The agents did tell us not to replace any carpets as they thought they were alright and to save our money.

Friday 19 December

The tenants move in today. We drive past the house for a nosey and see the removal van outside unloading. We can see the neighbour's curtains twitching.

We can't believe that we have bought and renovated a house and rented our old one out all in less than one year. What a year it has been. Wonder how long now before we decide to move again.

Glossary

Accompanied viewing –
The front door is unlocked take what you want/ the agent is watching every step you take

Estate Agent/Agent –
Selling your house is completed with minimum effort at a maximum price

Estate living –
Shiny cars with blacked out windows driving too fast, pastel coloured clothes, children with no manners AKA zombie world

For Sale Board –
Plaything of the local gang or drunks

Google Earth –
A gossip's dream come true

HIPs –
Where you pay loads of money for the privilege of a nosey person to look around your house

House brochure –
Containing the airbrushing skills of the house world where the photographer has to be a contortionist to make the pictures look good for the house brochure

Mortgage adviser –
Vary greatly, ranging from the good, the bad and the ugly who like to play god by deciding how much money to give you

New build sites –
Lego land for grown ups

Open house –
Like an accompanied viewing but can't steal anything because the vendor is in charge

Part exchange –
A quick way to sell your house or also known as an insult regarding the price you are offered

Post Office –
Where you join a queue for hours not knowing what is at the front all the time shuffling slowly, zombie world again with the post master behind a glass screen so he can't be beaten around the head for being a twat

Sales negotiator –
Person who hates you making money on your house sale when they never have, except ours because she was handpicked for the job from a previous dual

Sealed bids –
A leap of faith, let the Holy Spirit guide you

Solicitors –
Yours or theirs, friend or foe?

Valuation –
How cheap can the estate agents market your property, how little can they convince you what your house is worth in the current market

Valuer –
Sharp suit, big words, no reflection in shiny surfaces

Vendor –
Person who usually wants more than their property is worth in any market

Moving house checklist and jobs to do

<u>Who to notify with change of address</u>

Suppliers

- ➢ Gas
- ➢ Electric
- ➢ Water
- ➢ Telephone

Doctors/Dentist

TV Licence

Sky

Schools

Insurers – car/house/pet/life

Banks/Building Society

All cards, credit, debit, store cards – empty your purse out for this job, you won't forget anyone this way

Change of address cards – get out your address book when writing these cards, this is a good time to edit your contacts and not tell certain people you are moving

Neighbours – if you like them

Kennels/cattery

There may be more, the list really does go on and on …..

Moving checklist

Get the pets booked in with the kennels/cattery when you have a date booked for moving.

Get quotes from removal companies if you aren't doing the move with friends and family with their van.

If you are using a removal company they will give you boxes, tape and paper for packing

If you aren't using a removal company then go and collect loads of boxes from the supermarket, banana boxes are highly recommended as they are sturdy and have handle holes in the side. Also start collecting newspaper for packing. These boxes also do away with the need for packaging tape.

Defrost freezer and clean out fridge and freezer, even if you are leaving this for your buyers.

Remember to use up all food in the weeks before moving so you don't have to pay to move it to the new house, you can buy more food when you have moved in.

Moving day supplies box

Keep this box with you in your car when you move so it is handy and not lost in the depths of the removal van.

- ✓ Food/snacks
- ✓ Cutlery/crockery (plastic/paper is good for this, not granny's best stuff)
- ✓ Tea/coffee/milk/sugar
- ✓ Kettle
- ✓ Pop
- ✓ Mugs and beakers (again not Granny's best stuff)
- ✓ Many biscuits with a full and varied range to keep people happy
- ✓ Toilet roll
- ✓ Soap
- ✓ Towels, for bathrooms and kitchen
- ✓ Washing up liquid
- ✓ Kitchen roll
- ✓ Any medication
- ✓ Bedding – yours and the pets, you will not want to share with your pets on moving in day night!
- ✓ Keys
- ✓ Camera
- ✓ Purses/wallets
- ✓ Torch
- ✓ Matches

- ✓ Candles
- ✓ Pen
- ✓ I-pod/docking station with a banging playlist to keep workers happy

<u>Meter readings</u>

Remember to take these at your old house before you lock up for the last time and as soon as you get to your new house.

- ➤ Gas
- ➤ Electric
- ➤ Water

Useful websites

www.rightmove.co.uk

www.zoopla.co.uk

www.upmystreet.com

http://www.direct.gov.uk/en/HomeAndComm
unity/BuyingAndSellingYourHome/SellingY
ourHome/DG_10018035

https://www.royalmail.com/delivery/inbound-
mail/redirections

<u>Note to self</u>

9 781781 762257